She wore only his threadbare T-shirt and a blindfold

Desperately wanting to break the atmosphere of anticipation, Devon lifted the shirt slightly, and was rewarded with the sound of Jake's appreciative groan.

"You're leading off, Devon," he chastised, still milking the baseball analogy he'd started.

Devon licked her lips. "Isn't that the signal you sent me?"

"Don't anticipate my signals," he growled playfully. "Just my kiss, my hands. That, you see, is one of the keys to eroticism. Not knowing, but wondering, guessing. Just like a pitcher who has the other team's winning run on third base."

"Third base? What happened to first base?" Devon quipped.

Suddenly she heard the coffee table creak. Had Jake stood? She heard a tear of foil. A snap of...latex? This man sure took his game seriously and had all the right equipment close at hand.

"I think we covered first and second base in the stairwell the other day," Jake whispered in her ear, his breath causing a shiver to run down her spine. A shiver of want. Of need. "But the real skill, Devon, is sliding into third. And then—" he trailed a finger up her thighs "—stealing home."

Dear Reader,

It happens every time. I'm signing books in a mall, and some guy, who thinks he's incredibly original, comes up and asks, "Need any help with the research? *Hee, hee, hee.*"

My answer? "No thanks. I've got a husband." Sarcastic? Maybe. True? *Hee, hee, hee.* What do you think?

The truth is, a good writer has to draw on her personal experiences in order to make her story come to life. My heroine, mystery novelist Devon Michaels, has just figured this out, realizing that to research her next book, an *erotic* thriller, she'll need some help from sexy-as-sin cop Jake Tanner. You remember Jake, don't you? He's the taciturn partner of Cade Lawrence, the hero from *Just Watch Me...* (Blaze #29). Only, he's not so reserved anymore. It seems there's this mystery writer he has the hots for....

I'd love to hear what you think of *What's Your Pleasure?* You can drop me a line at P.O. Box 270885, Tampa, FL 33688-0885, or check out my Web site, www.julieleto.com, to get a sneak peek at my next Blaze novel, part of a two-book concurrent series I'm writing with Susan Kearney.

Have a hot and happy summer,

Julie Elizabeth Leto

Books by Julie Elizabeth Leto

HARLEQUIN TEMPTATION
686—SEDUCING SULLIVAN
724—PRIVATE LESSONS
783—GOOD GIRLS DO!
814—PURE CHANCE
835—INSATIABLE

HARLEQUIN BLAZE
4—EXPOSED
29—JUST WATCH ME...

WHAT'S YOUR PLEASURE?
Julie Elizabeth Leto

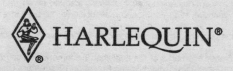

HARLEQUIN®

TORONTO • NEW YORK • LONDON
AMSTERDAM • PARIS • SYDNEY • HAMBURG
STOCKHOLM • ATHENS • TOKYO • MILAN • MADRID
PRAGUE • WARSAW • BUDAPEST • AUCKLAND

For Virginia Henley, who always encourages me
as a writer and inspires me as a reader.

For Cheryl Anne Porter, from whom I borrowed Sydney's line
that to write a good love scene..."First you need to have had
a love scene—and second, you need to have enjoyed it."

For Alexandria Kendall, whose desire to publish other
women's "Secrets" motivated me to imagine my own.

And for Tim Klapka, husband, friend
and consummate research partner.

ISBN 0-373-25984-0

WHAT'S YOUR PLEASURE?

Copyright © 2002 by Julie Leto Klapka.

Visit us at www.eHarlequin.com

Printed in U.S.A.

_____Prologue_____

THE BODY SPRAWLED on the pavement should have been her first priority—"should have" being the key phrase. But the minute her nemesis walked into her line of sight, all bets were off. Despite her years on the force and her success as a private investigator, Leah could never deny that she was a woman first and foremost—impossibly hot-blooded, incorrigibly on the prowl. How could a woman like her possibly keep her eyes on a dead collection of broken bones and torn muscle when such a prime live specimen—all male in all the right places—was headed her way?

"So, are you getting what you wanted?"

Devon Michaels blinked twice, glancing up from her notes just as Jake Tanner accomplished the seemingly impossible task of folding himself into the cafeteria chair. Not that the standard-issue plastic orange chair was particularly small. Detective Jake Tanner, a man much more potently male than any Devon could ever dream up in her fiction, was just so incredibly...large. Over six foot six of rough-and-tumble man, topped with a mane of rich, dark hair and eyes the color of fine Kentucky bourbon—precisely the combination of male perfection that made Devon Michaels, accomplished mystery author and teacher, stumble for words.

"Excuse me?"

Devon closed her notebook and clicked the top of her pen, hoping her grin didn't look too goofy. He'd interrupted her attempt to get a jump on chapter five of her current work in progress during the break at the Community Police Academy class he taught. She didn't mind the intrusion. She garnered her best inspiration while in the presence—usually the distant presence—of her instructor. The book was supposed to be, after all, an erotic thriller, and Devon's thoughts turned immediately to all things sensual the minute Jake Tanner stepped into a room.

Unfortunately, when the man entered her personal space, her thoughts turned to some odd mishmash of hems and haws. He apparently possessed the power to time warp her back seventeen years or so, when sharing breathing space with a handsome guy could steal her ability to form a coherent thought.

And now her breathing space intoxicated her with the scent of Old Spice and black coffee. What did he ask again?

"The photographs." Detective Tanner scooted toward her one of the dozen crime-scene snapshots she'd asked to borrow during the break. He chose one of the least shocking, though Devon had long ago developed immunity to pictures of blood and gore. If she could only develop an imperviousness to sexy, swaggering cops, she wouldn't be fighting a brain overload in order to answer his question.

He obviously read her befuddled expression as a request for clarification. "Are they helping you on your new book?"

Not half as much as you could help me...if I had the nerve to ask you.

"I haven't gotten a chance to really look at them yet," she answered.

Jake shrugged, and with the size of his shoulders, Devon was certain the movement caused a warm wind to blow toward her, spurring a hot little quiver over her skin. Either that, or the serious case of lust she'd been denying for six weeks was getting harder to ignore.

"It's interesting, having you in my class," he continued. "A mystery writer with your reputation—and following. You've got quite a few fans in the class."

Devon nodded and bit her lip. "I've been very lucky."

"So..." He drew the word out, as if he couldn't decide if he should ask the question swimming in his eyes. His take-charge personality seemingly won out with hardly a battle. "Why are you taking the course now? You already know a great deal about police procedure."

The moisture in Devon's mouth evaporated with each word he spoke. She realized for the first time that the man wasn't just being polite or curious. He wanted to have a conversation. A real exchange of information—beyond small talk.

Okay, she could do this. She was an adult. Boy, was she ever an adult. She'd waved goodbye to twenty-nine twice already. She'd interviewed countless vice and homicide detectives, several local police chiefs, the head of the Florida Department of Law Enforcement, the chief investigator on the FBI's task force on organized crime and even, because her famous sister loved pulling strings just to prove she could, the head of the Secret Service and the CIA.

And none of them had left her tongue-tied.

None of them spurred hot flashes or a tingling in her breasts, either.

Sexual attraction. What a concept.

"I like to keep up with what's current. You don't mind all the questions I ask, do you?"

Jake rewarded her query with a grin, causing a warm pool to form in her belly. The man had a grin best described as lopsided, reminding her of a young boy who'd just been paid an outrageous compliment. Humble pie, served with cinnamon apples and a big dollop of whipped cream.

Yum.

Only Jake Tanner was no young boy. She guessed he'd kissed twenty-nine goodbye at least five or six times by now, judging by the crinkly crow's-feet at the corners of his eyes and the sprinkling of gray throughout his incredibly thick, remarkably wavy hair.

"No, I don't mind at all," he answered. "And I think the class enjoys our...interaction."

He paused. Devon replayed what he'd said, then realized he'd planted an innuendo there for her to react to. So what was she supposed to say? That she'd enjoy some more interaction in private?

Devon snagged her diet soda and took a big sip. She was grinning like an idiot, she was sure. But if she'd learned one thing from her sister, the media-savvy rock star, it was that when you don't want to answer a question—don't. Just smile and look cute. Devon might not pull off the cute part as easily as Darcy, but she could do the smile, couldn't she?

Apparently not. Jake's brow furrowed, then he shook his head and continued. "Writers think a lot like detectives. We have an odd perspective, as if we..."

"Think backward!" Aha! A topic she could handle. "That's what my friend Sydney calls it. We start with an ending and work our way back."

Endings. Devon loved those almost as much as she loved a frozen Snickers bar on a hot day or hot fudge brownie sundaes with homemade vanilla ice cream and extra cherries. She loved those treats almost as much as she loved the fantasy of sharing that particular concoction with Detective Jake Tanner.

They only had two weeks of class left, and this was the first time she'd spoken to him outside polite hellos and the regular question-and-answer portion of the class. Of course, she had not initiated this conversation, nor had she sent a deliberate signal to welcome it. But she couldn't be so sure about any subliminal hints she might be broadcasting. Her inexperience kept her at a disadvantage in that department. She recognized her attraction to Jake Tanner—what living, breathing woman wouldn't react to the incredible force of the man's intense magnetism? But she had too many good and valid reasons for shying away.

For now, but not for much longer.

So, as per her normal mode of operation, Devon had isolated herself in a corner table of the old cafeteria while her classmates and their instructor enjoyed canned sodas and candy bars from the decades-old machines. Not that she didn't like socializing with the rest of the class—she always arrived early to chitchat with Mrs. Perez and her friends from Seminole Heights, the old Tampa neighborhood where they ran the Neighborhood Watch. Or to talk about haircuts and manicure techniques with Shawna Fielding, a stylist taking the class to alleviate some of her fears about her husband Mike's job as a patrolman. Devon had even admitted to Dirk and Sam, two teenagers considering the academy as a career, that she was, as they suspected, the sister of current MTV diva D'Arcy Wilde, which of course led to the inevitable request for autographs, which she had delivered this morning.

For six weeks, she'd been avoiding talking with Detective Tanner except during class. Personal dialogue could lead to the discovery that she liked him more than she already suspected. That she wanted him more than she already suspected. That denying her heart's desire was a cowardly act rather than a selfless one.

She couldn't afford the complication of a love affair in her life—yet. But soon. Maybe. After her niece, Cassie, left for the summer next week. After she had her current book contract signed, sealed and delivered, along with the much anticipated and much needed seven-figure advance. After she found a way to make sure any relationship wouldn't result in her falling in love.

Soon, she'd be a single woman with no responsibilities beyond those to herself. She'd spent her entire life taking care of other people, putting everyone else's needs before hers. But soon, she'd be truly on her own, able for the first time to figure out who she was and what she wanted, particularly where Jake, and any other man for that matter, was concerned.

Jake snapped her out of her thoughts by reaching over and toying with the metal coil of her notebook. "I don't know much about writing books but, yeah, detectives have to think backward. Never thought of it that way before. Start with the crime and work their way to motive and opportunity. That's an interesting concept."

Devon nodded, rolling her lips while she marveled at the size of Jake's hands, the length of his strong fingers, the calluses he'd undoubtedly earned from hours of target practice with his gun, a 9mm Glock, she guessed, from the spacing and shape of the hardened skin on his knuckles. And, once again, she noted the absence of a ring. Devon had cataloged that particular lack of jewelry on the first day of class six weeks ago and had confirmed Jake's single status, unbidden of course, with Mrs. Perez soon after.

He was single. She was single. They were both adults. Even her inexperience didn't keep her from recognizing that Jake's interest in her wasn't limited to her theories on fiction.

That thought caused her to grab her notebook and pull it against her chest.

Jake frowned. "I don't suppose you'd like to discuss our strange thought processes further—over dinner, maybe?"

His voice, essentially monotone, spoke volumes to Devon, a keen listener. He expected her to say no.

God, she was an idiot.

"This is a really busy time for me right now."

He nodded and stood.

She'd tried not to decline his offer entirely, but somehow she'd dismissed him. *Stupid, stupid, stupid!* She'd told him the truth. What more could she say without sounding desperate?

"Maybe some other time, then," he said. "You can keep the pictures. Unfortunately, I have more."

He turned on his grin at a painfully low wattage, then stalked out of the room.

Devon swore, then stuffed her notebook into her purse, knowing she wouldn't write another word today. She dragged out some change and stomped to the candy machine. The Snickers weren't cold, but they were chocolate. And that was the important part.

Maybe some other time, he'd said. Maybe when she'd somehow overcome her inability to think about herself before everyone else. Like Cassie. And Darcy. Maybe after she stopped running from the things that truly frightened her—like Jake Tanner thinking she was a fascinating and mysterious author when she was really just a woman who'd denied her own needs for far too long.

Yeah, maybe.

1

THE SEX isn't doing it for me.

Devon reread the sentence on the faxed letter, briefly wondering if the phrase would bother her less if it had been written by a lover rather than by her book editor. Problem was, she hadn't had a lover in, oh, what? Five years?

So the answer was, no, she would not be bothered less. For the last decade, she'd devoted herself to two things—raising her niece while her rock-star sister toured the world, and building her career as a novelist. And now her inexperience in the sex department was becoming a serious impediment to her breaking out of the mystery midlist and into the bestseller big time.

The image of Jake Tanner popped into her mind. Sex with him would probably do it for her, her editor, her agent and the entire free world. But she'd turned him down. Well, put him off. She'd sent him a gift a few days later, crossing her fingers that she'd undone any damage her refusal had caused. Lord, how she'd wanted to say yes! And she would. Soon.

"Devon, you there?"

She adjusted the earpiece on her telephone's headset, having forgotten for a moment she was on the line with Mel. "Oh, yeah. Sorry, Mel. I've got the revisions from the editor right here. Thanks for faxing them so fast."

"Anything you can't do?"

Devon didn't bother trying to scan four single-spaced pages of proposed changes—mainly to the love scene she'd submitted—while her agent, fast-track bulldog Mel Bruskin, waited. He'd hang up if she paused too long. Time was, after all, money.

"I can do anything, right?" she answered.

"You'd better. We've got a million-dollar deal on the table, Devon."

With that, he disconnected the call. She didn't need him to remind her about the money or hold her hand throughout the writing process. She'd hired him for one purpose and one purpose only—to sell her work to the highest bidder for the highest price. He'd taken less than two weeks to negotiate a potential deal that could ensure Devon's financial independence from her sister—a million-plus advance for a hardcover breakout bestseller from the mystery genre's current paperback darling.

Only the publisher didn't want another of Devon's witty cozies where her seventy-three-year-old hero-ine, fading Mafia princess Fioranna DiMarco, stumbled into a nasty crime she invariably solved. They wanted the wit but not the "old broad." Their words. They wanted young, hip, sexy.

Emphasis on sexy.

They wanted a romantic suspense—or better yet, an

erotic thriller. When Mel had called with the offer, Devon of the I-can-do-anything mind-set had no qualms accepting the challenge, even if it meant jumping with both feet outside her personal comfort zone. She could write a love scene. Sure. Why not? She'd had a love scene or two in her life. Or was it one? Definitely one. Sort of. Okay, the encounter was more like a delayed lust explosion with a former boyfriend from high school after an unexpected reunion. Only lust explosion didn't quite capture the interlude, either. More like a hormone high followed by a fast fizzle.

She planned to have another love scene real soon with a man who could teach her a thing or two, but she hadn't counted on needing him to help sell her book.

"Hey, Aunt Devon! Syd's here!" bellowed a voice from downstairs.

Devon grimaced at her niece's brand of formal announcement of a visitor. Well, what could she expect from a seventeen-year-old? Besides, after Saturday, she'd no longer have her niece's foibles to lighten her days. Nor would she have Cassie's sharp drollery and award-winning snuggle hugs to shrink the house from a monster mansion to a cozy home. Devon blinked back tears. She'd cried like Niagara Falls all last week. She couldn't deal with the headaches her jags caused anymore—she was out of Tylenol.

She fanned her hands over her eyes and forced herself to act as if there was nothing unusual or out of the

ordinary in the fact that Cassie was about to leave.
Teenagers became adults. They grew up. They moved
away. They went to college out of state, even if Devon
had willingly given up that dream the day eleven-
month-old Cassie said her name before anyone else's.

An De-bon. Aunt Devon.

She choked back a sob.

Devon tapped the intercom button by the phone in
her home office. "Ask Syd to come up, please."

Naturally, Sydney was already crossing the threshold, looking way too gorgeous for someone who'd
just biked the ten miles between her house and
Devon's. Except for a few spots of sweat soaking her
emerald-green spandex tank top and black bike
shorts, Devon's redheaded friend seemed fresh as an
Irish rose and ready to take on the world.

"The kid's got lungs like her mother. She should be
singing."

Devon took off the headset, leaned over to the cof-
feepot on the credenza and poured Sydney a cup. "If
my sister has anything to say about it, Cassie will be
taking the stage sometime during this tour. She'll be
the first singing physicist in the history of the Nobel
Prize."

Sydney laughed, tossing her empty water bottle
into Devon's recycle bin before grabbing the mug.
"When do they leave?"

Devon shook her head and grimaced, wondering
again how Darcy and Cassie were going to keep from
killing each other without her there to show them

how to get along. She'd raised her sister's daughter by example and by modeling good behavior after reading somewhere that that was the best technique. Darcy wasn't so effective at it, too often buying into the rock-star diva mentality.

My way or the highway. Her favorite phrase.

But luckily, Cassie often managed to be the adult when her mother couldn't hack it. Devon had to bank on Cassie coming through yet again. She'd spend the summer touring with her mother in Europe but, in the fall, she'd begin her freshman year at Tulane University with a full scholarship to study physics.

And that would leave Devon, for the first time in the eighteen years since Cassie's birth, with all the time in the world to focus on herself and her personal goals.

And needs. Can't forget those needs.

"Darcy left for London last night," Devon said. "Cassie wanted to stay for graduation, so she'll leave after the ceremony on Friday."

Sydney didn't drink until she'd added enough nonfat cream and sugar substitute to qualify the concoction as some crazy calorie-free dessert. "Darcy couldn't take two days out of being the center of the universe to attend her own daughter's graduation?"

Devon shrugged. "You're surprised?"

"You know, your sister's a certified, self-centered... star." Sydney wiggled her eyebrows and grinned, apparently proud of herself for not saying anything more vulgar, for once. "This is not news."

"Least of all to Cassie. She said she didn't want Darcy at graduation."

"There's trouble?"

Syd scooted a pillow across the futon where Devon had been spending way too many nights lately...and afternoons, and mornings...daydreaming and fantasizing and reading everything from classic erotica to *Penthouse Forum* while listening to everyone from Prince to George Michael to Kenny G. She'd been hoping to generate ideas on how to spice up her writing, but so far, she'd been as successful at capturing the nuances of sensual literature as her sister had been at parenting.

Not good.

If not for the occasional, spine-tingling fantasy starring Detective Jake Tanner, Devon would have given up entirely. But those fantasies were for her—not for her book. Right?

She clutched the faxed revision letter a little tighter, then slapped it, facedown, on her desk.

"No trouble, really," she answered. "Cassie loves Darcy, and vice versa. But Cassie has survived an absentee mother by creating very controlled compartments in her life." Devon used her hands, bent into neat squares, to illustrate. "School is here. Home is here. Friends are here. Mom is somewhere way over there. So long as none of the compartments spill over, she's a very happy kid."

"Compartments, huh? Wonder where she learned that survival tactic?" Sydney sang her supposition in just the right tone to point a finger at Devon. Compartmentalizing had proved to be an invaluable way to handle her life, at least until now.

She'd been only fifteen when her seventeen-year-old sister had come home with a positive pregnancy test in one hand and an offer to sing backup for a popular local club band in the other. Their mother, a single parent with a giving heart and frail health, had shaken her head and promised to help Darcy any way she could. Devon had done her part, scheduling her high school and college classes around the baby's schedule, taking on all household chores so her mother could reserve her energy for Cassie. Devon had become Cassie's legal guardian when their mother died, only three weeks after Cassie turned five and Darcy accepted an offer to go solo with a major record label.

So Devon had learned to fence in her emotions, corral her disappointments and categorize all aspects of her life into neatly packed shoe boxes she could deal with separately and one at a time. Sydney had never been able to understand the benefits of being organized and logical.

Sydney Colburn—"Slow-Burn Colburn" to her legion of readers and fans—had more self-confidence and good old-fashioned chutzpah than anyone Devon had ever met in her thirty-something years on this planet. Sydney flew by the seat of her pants with great success and pretty much believed her way could work for everyone.

Despite their differences, Devon had gravitated toward the outspoken woman in a college creative writing class, and they'd been best pals ever since. Devon was all logic and order. Sydney was emotion and chaos. But, hey, it worked somehow. Devon embraced the time-honored logic of not fixing what wasn't broken. Besides, she enjoyed having an alternative perspective in her life.

However, Devon's new deal *was* going to be broken if she didn't get a handle on writing a truly compelling love scene—something that stood out as fresh and new and downright steamy. She glanced at the revision letter.

She was in so much trouble.

"Maybe once you're alone in this big old house," Sydney said, "you'll get serious about writing this crap you call erotic."

On cue, Sydney pulled a mangled collection of paper, practically dripping with purple ink, her favorite color for critique, from her backpack. Since Syd had been on deadline and couldn't read for her beforehand, Devon had sent the proposal to Syd at the same time she'd sent it to the editor. Obviously, neither of them had been impressed.

Devon accepted the chapter cautiously, by a corner, between two pinched fingers. "Wow, you loved it that much, huh?"

She was tempted to toss it in the garbage but knew her friend was trying to help. And, Lord knew, she needed the assistance.

Sydney and she had been working together for years, editing and critiquing each other's work even before they'd both sold. But never before had Devon crossed into Sydney's territory. Sydney wrote sizzling-hot historical sagas set in the bawdy Elizabethan period. Devon had spent many, many hours distracted and enthralled by the lusty, wild sex in Sydney's books, often forgetting she was supposed to be checking for bad grammar. She'd often dreamed she could one day be like one of Sydney's heroines, all redheaded hellions or raven-haired shrews who somehow managed to tame the darkest knights and most dangerous pirates to win the reward of true love.

As a writer, Devon had considered herself lucky she didn't have to spend weeks in a stuffy corner of the library researching monarchical political coups or underwear styles from the sixteenth century. Sure, she spent plenty of time digging up information on criminal investigations and the multitude of ways to murder someone without leaving obvious evidence, but that was more interesting than corsets and cod-pieces, right?

She wasn't so sure anymore.

"Devon, honey, you're in big trouble here." Sydney crossed her ankle over her knee and swigged her drink. "Right now, I'd say you are in way over your head. Have you heard from the editor yet?"

Devon traded the purple-inked manuscript for the fax.

Syd scanned the missive, nodding as she read. "Yup, I agree. The sex sure as hell didn't do it for me, either."

"Well, then, it's unanimous."

"Meaning the sex didn't titillate you at all?"

"Of course it didn't!"

"Well, dammit, Devon, that's the whole problem! Don't you think I get all hot and bothered when I write those rowdy romps? I finished a particularly luscious scene yesterday morning. Let's just say that my neighbor upstairs is now one very happy man."

"You're doing it with your neighbor upstairs? He's like, what, ten years old?"

Sydney wiggled her pencil-thin eyebrows. "He's twenty-three but could be eighteen for all I care. If he can afford the condo above mine, then he can help me work off some sexual energy. Someone like him is just what you need."

"A rich boy toy?"

Sydney's grin was pure sin. "Rich, poor, young, old—doesn't matter, babe. You need a man. I've always said there are only two things a writer needs to write a good love scene. First, she needs to have personally experienced a love scene, and second, she needs to have enjoyed it. You and I both know you don't qualify."

"Lord, Syd, do we have to go there again?"

Her friend responded by waving the rejection letter in her face. "Exactly how many more times do you think they're going to ask you to revise before they revoke this offer? It's not a done deal. That bulldog agent of ours isn't going to go to the mat for you if you can't come through. You need editorial approval of the proposal before they shell out the big advance, right?"

Devon nodded, knowing her editor had been extremely patient so far, mainly because the woman had edited one of Devon's first mysteries when she worked for another publishing house years ago. And this last proposal had been Devon's second unsuccessful attempt. Sooner or later, patience would run out. Publishing was a business, and publishers wanted to make money a hell of a lot more than they wanted to spend it. If they intended to spend a million dollars to buy Devon Michaels's name, then they needed a hot product to recoup that expense.

"So, what do I do to improve my love scenes? It's not like there are any men living in my attic. I can't run upstairs for a quickie."

"Baby, you need a quickie like I need a hole in the head. You need a slow sizzle. A controlled burn. You need a real man, one who knows some things about real loving. Someone who will help you get your passion perfect."

"Passion perfect? Sounds like a new verb tense," Devon quipped, trying not to think about Jake. Jake wasn't for the book. Jake was for her.

"Oh, it is, honey," Sydney sang, her voice as deep and throaty as that of any soulful songstress, "it most certainly is." Syd punctuated her intimation by licking her lips.

Devon threw her hands up in surrender. Syd was right. Devon didn't need to do anything drastic to achieve her goals. She just needed a good, old-fashioned love affair. No, scratch that. She needed a good, new-generation love affair.

No commitments. No expectations. As much as she was going to miss her niece, Devon had put off her freedom for way too long. She needed time on her own. Time to stretch her wings, test her ability to flourish by herself and for herself. The last thing she needed was to jump from the responsibilities of pseudo-motherhood into the responsibilities of a serious relationship. Or marriage.

Devon had no trouble with the concept of marriage, even if she'd never been personally exposed to the institution. Her father had disappeared before her birth, not that he'd ever bothered to make his relationship with her mother legal. Her sister had been married once, briefly—so briefly Devon couldn't remember the guy's name. Even Sydney, for all her romantic notions and thrilling affairs, had never taken the ultimate plunge.

But marriage seemed a lifetime away for Devon, despite that she'd long passed the average age for becoming a bride. In many ways, Devon felt like a teenager, since she'd never had a chance to be much of one in real life. So if she did follow Sydney's advice, as she was inclined to, she had to make sure she found a man who didn't want gold rings or shared bank accounts in his immediate future.

"A man well versed in the passion perfect, huh?" Devon mused, pushing away the supposition that Jake could fulfill her needs. Having an affair with him would be like entering an Olympic gymnastic event before she'd done her first cartwheel.

But she had sent him that gift. Gotten the ball rolling, so to speak.

"Anyone cute in your writing class?" Syd asked.

Devon shook her head. She'd told no one about Jake's invitation, her refusal or her makeup present. As usual, she'd placed her attraction to Jake in a separate strongbox from the rest of her life. She hadn't considered the possibility of breaking down the barriers and connecting all the dots.

She answered Sydney while mulling the possibility. "The current crop contains five men, total—two who still treat their acne every morning, two who would need Viagra and one who is in love with a bus driver named Gus. Not that they aren't all darling, but..."

"But no potential Mr. Goodbars." Sydney remained silent while she drank the rest of her coffee. "What about that community police course you're taking? Didn't you mention the instructor was some hot stuff?"

"Detective Tanner?"

Devon swallowed deeply, not surprised Sydney would zone in so quickly on the man she'd tried to keep secret. She wondered when she might have discussed Jake with Sydney but gave up trying to pin-point the exact conversation. Every Tuesday night, they played poker, drank frozen froufrou drinks and spilled all sorts of secrets. Even if Devon had made only a passing comment, Sydney had a sexual radar comparable to a CIA tracking device. Trying to hide matters relating to lust from her would be a fruitless endeavor.

Still, Devon's logical side dictated that she should begin her sexual education on a smaller scale—with a soft-spoken, sweet, maybe shy man who would tend her needs and teach her. Slowly. She could work her way up to a god like Jake Tanner.

But her logical side hadn't been the one who'd sent him that provocative present, had it? No, she'd done that after a pitcherful of Midori Sours, a straight flush, two three-of-a-kinds and one sleepless night.

The man was a drop-dead gorgeous giant. Solidly built, sinfully handsome. She imagined he had to hand stretch the little cuffy things on the arms of his Tampa Police Department polo shirt so they wouldn't cut off the circulation to his tremendous biceps.

And his eyes...whiskey colored and deeply set, like two faceted topaz stones in a thick gold nugget ring. Beautiful, but rugged and tough. Like his mouth. He didn't smile much, except for a self-deprecating grin that always lifted higher on the left side of his mouth.

She didn't bother to contain a dreamy sigh with only Syd to witness.

"Oh, yeah." Syd leaned back into the futon and

laced her hands behind her head, triumphant. "Lordy, Dev, but you blushed after just saying his name! This Detective Tanner is the one."

The one. Devon couldn't deny that the man haunted her dreams, even if she'd been unsuccessful at transferring her fantasy onto paper. Maybe a little physical interaction, a little reality, could break down the wall of her writer's block. He was, after all, interested.

Devon shook her head, snapping her mind clear before any fantasies had a chance to form. Detective Tanner had indeed been the model for the love interest in her book proposal, though she'd carefully hidden his identity by making him bleached blond with blue eyes and cutting his height by eight inches. Not exactly her type, but the cop in her story and the cop who taught her class were both, well, cops.

She crinkled her nose. Maybe she needed to give the character a little tweak. She'd been so worried about revealing her personal attraction to Detective Tanner that she'd made his fictional alter ego as far from the real man as she could. Not that she had anything against stocky, bleached-blond blue-eyed men— they just didn't turn her on the way muscle-bound mountains like Detective Tanner did.

"I can't seduce him for the book, Syd."

"Why the hell not?"

"Um, because that would be *using* him," Devon answered, her hesitation only for effect.

Sydney's stare reminded Devon of the time she'd

given instructions in Spanish to her Portuguese-speaking lawn man. Talking to Syd about the morality of using someone for sex was the equivalent of speaking another language.

"Let's skip that argument," Devon suggested. "In fact, let's skip this whole discussion."

Even though Syd's idea had merit on several different levels, Devon wasn't sure she wanted Syd involved. Bringing her friend into the mix meant no backing out, no changing her mind.

Sydney reacted to Devon's reluctance with her usual frustration. She jumped to her feet. "Don't even bother giving me some line about him not knowing you're alive. You're a beautiful woman, Dev. Men find you attractive. They always have. You just never follow through."

Sydney wasn't exaggerating—about her attractiveness or her reluctance to pursue a man. Devon appreciated her luck in the looks department, but her resemblance to her older sister, the Grammy Award–winning D'arcy Wilde, aka Darcy Laverne Michaels, often colored her confidence. Devon didn't dye her already dark brown hair to onyx black or shade her dark blue eyes with sapphire kohl liner like Darcy did, but she'd been mistaken for her sister enough times to wonder if some guys just wanted a cheaper substitute.

Devon had dated a few times, and invariably the jerks seemed disappointed that she hadn't inherited her sister's obsession with black leather or her penchant for fast living. Devon preferred T-shirts and blue jeans. She liked renting movies and popping her own popcorn more than gluing herself into a ball gown to attend some glittery premiere. Practicing French manicures with her niece and gabbing over freshly brewed Maxwell House with Sydney were way more her style than fancy salons and trendy coffee bars.

She wondered if Jake knew who her sister was. He didn't seem the MTV type. More Bruce Springsteen than the Backstreet Boys. Fleetwood Mac. Maybe Steve Miller Band. And if she was lucky, Styx. But he was definitely VH-1.

Just like her.

"I'm pretty sure Detective Tanner finds me attractive," Devon said. "But that's personal. I don't want to use him just so I can sell my book."

"Being able to use a man for sex is the payment women have earned for years of being used themselves," Syd declared, waving her hand at Devon in a gesture that was so much like Darcy, Devon almost laughed. She'd learned her lesson about pointing out the similarities between her wild-child sister and her irreverent best friend. Last time, Syd hadn't spoken to her for a week. "Pure and simple physical attraction is all you need. And you need it bad."

"I'm not exactly starving, Syd. I'll survive if they pull the deal."

"Will you? You think another publisher will touch you with a big deal if you can't come through? Don't kid yourself, Devon. You've got to make this work. You have the talent. You have the drive. Now you just need the knowledge. Besides, with Cassie almost out of the house, I know you're not thrilled about taking your sister's handouts."

Devon leaned back in her chair and balanced her bare feet on the corner of her desk. "I've never been crazy about letting Darcy set me up in this house, but I didn't have a choice with Cassie to think of. She deserved the best."

She looked at her luxurious surroundings, a large home office on the second floor of the three-story mansion Darcy had bought with the proceeds from her first platinum album. Situated in the back of a well-guarded gated community, the house provided Darcy with all the security she needed when she came home for visits. A tall stone wall and a roving guard kept the paparazzi from capturing shots of the famous D'arcy Wilde's love child for the tabloids. The entire experience was a lifetime away from the double-wide trailer on an unpaved road Devon and Darcy had grown up in.

Devon had worked very hard to make the place warm and comfy—their home rather than a prison, a safe haven rather than a stuffy museum.

Her home. Eventually, she'd fallen in love with the solitude. Devon planned to use the book deal so she could buy the place from her sister and start paying her own way.

The symbolism didn't escape her. She understood

and accepted her need to prove herself—to herself, to her sister and to anyone and everyone who attributed her success as a novelist to her being related to a mega-star. Buying the house and breaking out of the midlist were the next reasonable steps in her quest for independence—steps she had to take on her own.

"You're going to be lonely here, you know that, right?" Sydney added, as if Devon needed reminding.

"I love this house, Syd. Besides, the book will distract me...even though writing it, so far, has been pure torture."

"Torture can be a good thing," Sydney claimed, her brows wiggling, "particularly if your Detective Tanner is working the whips and chains."

Devon forced a laugh and shook her head but silently trembled with a forbidden thrill. Surrendering to Syd's suggestion wasn't so hard when she admitted to herself, even in the tiniest, hard-to-hear voice, that she'd found the perfect motivation to follow through and go after a man she truly desired, a man who made her heart pound and her breasts tingle simply by looking in her direction. And Devon always needed a reason—a good, logical one—to put her personal needs at the forefront of her life. Her sexual desires had been kept in check for a long time, and uncorking her passions might be downright dangerous if she didn't keep her eye on the prize.

The book contract.

She had class on Saturday afternoon, just after she took Cassie to the airport for her flight to London.

Sometime before then, she'd figure out how to properly seduce her fantasy man and lure him to teach her the nuances of hot, passionate desire—with no strings attached.

2

ONCE THE LIGHTS flickered the third time, Jake knew his class was effectively over. For an hour, Mrs. Perez, seventy-five years old and the captain of her Neighborhood Watch, had been concentrating only on the sheets of rain pelting the old jalousie windows of the centrally located Adult High School building. The possibility of a power outage had her downright anxious. Her companions, Mr. Riegert and Mrs. Schaumberg, had been ignoring his slide show on TRT and SWAT procedures, talking nervously to each other as reverberating blasts of thunder drowned his explanations of covert operations. Even the anatomy skeleton hanging in the corner shimmied and swayed.

The younger members of the class, two wives trying to understand their patrolman husbands' jobs and three teenagers considering the academy, also worriedly watched the weather. This was more than a typical Florida afternoon downpour. Living in the lightning capital of the world during an electrical storm made even the natives restless.

Including Devon Michaels. Jake wasn't sure if the weather was entirely responsible, but the mystery author who'd turned down his request for a date last week and then surprised him with a provocative gift had the word *restless* written all over her—from her sexy, unbuttoned-to-the-cleavage blouse and skin-tight jeans to her thickly lashed blue eyes.

"Let's cut class a little short today," Jake suggested, switching off his projector. The room seemed to swell with one big sigh of relief, though his glance over at Devon's subtle grin caused a different kind of inflammation altogether.

Mrs. Perez clapped her hands. "Oh, thank goodness! I don't want to fight interstate traffic in this deluge to get home." She gathered her notebook and her cross-stitch project into a large straw bag. "Come on, dear," she said to Mr. Riegert, who wiggled his unruly brows at Jake while he allowed the woman to help him stand. Even though he was probably the healthiest of the three, the old coot enjoyed the clucking. "We can't be late for dinner or your blood sugar will go bonkers."

Jake shook his head in amused disbelief. "We wouldn't want that to happen. Be careful on the elevators. The power has blinked a few times, but the generators should hold." He would have suggested his elderly students take the stairs, but they were four stories up, and he knew for a fact that Mrs. Schaumberg's heart shouldn't take that much exercise. "We'll meet back here next week for graduation."

The class cleared out of the room quickly, the sound of rustling bags and shuffling feet nearly drowned by the downpour. Only after he disconnected the slide projector and flipped on the main lights did he notice that Devon hadn't made a single move to leave. Instead, she was staring at some notations in her slim notebook, her tongue lazily swiping back and forth across her top lip as she pondered whatever the hell she was pondering.

Back and forth. Slick tongue over pink lips. Like a swinging gold watch. Hypnotic. Alluring.

Jake cleared his throat. "Something bothering you, Ms. Michaels?"

She grinned softly before she looked up from beneath lashes just a tad darker and thicker than usual. Jake stood a little straighter. Whatever she'd changed about her makeup had done magic to her dark blue eyes. And he'd already noticed that she'd worn her hair differently. Usually, her nearly black hair was braided and secured with a colorless clip between her shoulder blades. Today, she'd softly twined only enough hair to pull the waves from her face, leaving the length free to hug her shoulders.

She wore her signature jeans and blouse, but this time he was certain the denim was a half size tighter, and the blouse—a sleeveless button-down tied at the waist—was unfastened just a bit more. And she wore earrings. Not her usual plain gold studs, but dangling baubles that glittered silver and turquoise, catching the gleam in her indigo eyes.

He wasn't certain if anything was bothering her, but he knew he was in one hell of a lust-induced fix.

"I was just thinking about those cold cases you told

us about at the beginning of class." She tapped the pen over her notes. "I'm sure there's a story or two in there."

Jake hadn't meant to share such a petty frustration with the class, but as usual, Mrs. Perez had coerced him into talking about his personal life. She always asked about his "project for the week." Hers had been cross-stitching a teddy bear plaque for her new great-grandbaby. Jake had too much respect for his elders to put her off, but he couldn't very well admit he'd spent the better part of the week under suspension from the force and getting personal with his good friend Jack Daniels. He also couldn't confess to an impressive series of erotic daydreams starring Devon Michaels, mystery author—the woman who'd put him off less than seven days ago, only to entice him with an autographed copy of her latest book.

Well, it wasn't the book that had enticed him, though he'd read it cover to cover, amazed at the complexity of the woman's mind. No, it had been the inscription that kept him off-kilter all week long.

Let's think backward. Thanks for last night, Devon.

She'd punctuated the missive with a kiss pressed to the thick paper in fiery red lipstick and spritzed with a sample of the alluring vanilla scent she wore.

No, he most definitely couldn't tell Mrs. Perez about how much time he'd spent sniffing that book, so he'd spilled about the five cold cases he was re-opening for further investigation.

And in doing so, he had obviously intrigued the object of his fantasies, a woman who apparently wanted to undo her refusal to go out with him. Piquing her interest with tales from his job hadn't been his plan, but Jake had been known to improvise on occasion.

"A story for your mystery novels? I don't know. There's only one dead body and no international conspiracies. And, unfortunately, no new clues."

"Ah, but you don't really know that for certain, do you? On the surface, they may seem to be two assaults, one grand theft, one hit-and-run and a suspected homicide, but what if they lead you to something much, much bigger? And even if they don't, I've gotten some of my best ideas from less than a snippet in the newspaper."

He nodded, impressed. She not only listened carefully and took great notes, but the way her eyes lit up when she spoke about mystery and mayhem turned him on, big time. The woman was smart, unafraid, and best of all, interested. So far, her interest extended only to his job and maybe dinner, but he could work with that.

The lightning and thunder clashed again, making her jump as she clicked her pen and closed her notebook.

"You okay?" he asked.

Devon eyed the storm warily. "As much as I try to appreciate the beauty of nature, I really hate thunderstorms. You'd think I'd be long used to this weather by now."

"Have you lived here all your life?"

Jake couldn't resist the opportunity to find out a little more about her—more than he could discover from the inside cover of her novel or the Web site hosted by an incredibly loyal core of fans. After spending a few hours on the message boards this week, following as they dissected her books with nearly unanimous praise, Jake knew a great deal about Devon Michaels the mystery writer.

But he'd learned next to nothing about Devon Michaels the woman. Unlike the writers he'd studied in high school and college, Ms. Michaels didn't reveal herself in her work. The recurring heroine in her books was pushing eighty, was Italian and rode around town in a limo that had once belonged to Al Capone—bullet holes and all.

Devon, on the other hand, was barely beyond thirty, of homogenized heritage and drove a pristine Cadillac Escalade that didn't even have a bumper sticker to reveal her politics or her sense of humor. The articles and letters she'd posted to the site dealt with the craft and theory of writing. Nothing about her wants, needs or desires.

Jake wasn't entirely disappointed. Left him topics to discuss with her one-on-one. A single turned-down dinner invitation wasn't enough to deter him, particularly after her handwritten note, sealed with a sweet kiss. Between last Saturday and this one, something had changed. And that was damned fine with him.

"I was born and raised in sunny Florida," she said with a smirk. "A dying breed. You?"

Jake couldn't resist a grin. "We may be the last two of our species." He stared at her a moment, allowing her to mull the implications of his statement.

The quick rise of one eyebrow testified that her wit was as sharply honed as a knife, as he suspected. He'd lobbed her an innuendo last week, one she'd opted not to return. But he'd seen the quip in her eyes, known she was biting her tongue.

"That could be an interesting scenario." She grinned, then winked.

Winked! Okay, Jake knew without a doubt that the woman was intentionally flirting, and the cop in him wanted to know why. The man in him told the cop to shut the hell up and go for it, but Jake knew he had to find a quick compromise between the two before he lost a golden opportunity—like some hint as to why *now*.

"You seem a little different today, Ms. Michaels. Friendlier, maybe?"

She slid out of her desk with such graceful undulation that Jake wondered how many of her male college professors had been enthralled by the move.

"Aren't I friendly every Saturday?"

Jake took a chance. "Yes, but you don't flirt with me every Saturday. And last Saturday you turned me down."

She faltered, but only for an instant. She quickly recouped from a nearly imperceptible stumble by unsnagging her purse from around her chair. She slipped the notebook and pen inside, then slung the

strap over her shoulder. After a deep breath, she began walking toward him.

"Didn't you receive the present I sent? And I didn't
exactly turn you down, detective. If you recall, I said
that the timing wasn't right." She closed her eyes, and
when she opened them, her mouth followed suit, re-
leasing a jumble of words Jake had to strain to understand. "But, frankly, my life has recently undergone a
huge change. My list of reasons I couldn't afford a
man in my life, even briefly, has disappeared, so I was
wondering if you'd like to go somewhere and grab an
early dinner?"

He waited for her to take another deep breath, certain she needed one after she pushed all those words
out in such a mad rush. She finally inhaled, and when
she exhaled, they both laughed.

"Sorry," she apologized, rolling her eyes. "I had to
get that all off my chest before I chickened out."

Jake chuckled and shook his head. He'd known
Devon Michaels long enough to figure out that the
woman was pretty, quietly sexy and incredibly smart.
But he hadn't expected her to be so refreshingly honest.

"I don't usually evoke fear in women," he told her,
surprised that her truthfulness had instantly spawned
the same response in him. Jake usually wore his emotions well protected beneath a bulletproof vest, not on
his sleeve for the world to see.

"Detective Tanner, I find that very hard to believe."
The lightning and thunder crashed once more in

unison, draining a little of the natural pink glow from Devon's face and prompting Jake to scoop up his stuff and gesture toward the door.

"I'd love to have dinner with you, but we'll have to take your car unless you want a soaking-wet companion. I rode my bike."

"You don't watch the weather reports, huh?"

Jake didn't answer, loath to admit he'd had a lot more on his mind this morning when he'd ridden his Yamaha to class rather than drive his big, bulky, unimpressive, unmarked police car. A man certainly couldn't impress a woman of Devon's caliber with a clunker like a four-door Chevy—not that he was winning any points by having to bum a ride.

He gestured toward the door, waiting for her to exit while he wrangled the keys from his pocket and locked the dead bolt. The hallway, shadowy from outdated lighting and the clouds outside, echoed with the sound of her footsteps. The thick clicks brought his attention to her incredibly small feet, encased in sexy black ankle boots with thin wedge heels.

She'd thought of everything—sexy from head to toe. Well, he wasn't sure she'd thought of *everything* everything, like seductive lingerie underneath her clothes. But he considered Victoria and her secret wares highly overrated anyway, though he certainly wouldn't object if Devon wore something lacy against her bare skin.

As she punched the button on the elevator, Jake cursed Mother Nature for sending a rainstorm when he wanted nothing more than to feel Devon mounted on his bike behind him, her face turned into the wind, her arms about his waist. He'd bought the bike about two years ago and rarely took it out of his carpeted garage except for an occasional midnight run up the highway to blow off steam. He'd never shared the experience with anyone, least of all a woman. And he couldn't help wondering what magic the quiet, intellectual Devon Michaels had cast to insert the image into his brain.

Whatever magic it was, Jake wanted more.

Another crash of lightning sent Devon a few inches into the air. She dropped her purse and wrapped her arms around herself, squealing when the electricity flickered again, then went dark.

Emergency lights flashed to life, sending dim beams in several directions.

"Devon?" he asked.

He heard her take a deep breath. "I'm okay. I hope everyone was off the elevator."

The light in the hallway had been shadowy, so his eyes adjusted quickly. He pressed his ear to the elevator door.

"It's quiet. They'd be screaming for help if they were stuck. They must have all gotten down before the power went off. Good thing we weren't on board or we'd be stuck right now."

"I don't know," Devon mused, leaning on the elevator doors next to him, "could have been one of those interesting scenarios again."

Jake gasped with amusement. "Ms. Michaels, you have one wicked mind."

"Detective Tanner, you have no idea."

No, he didn't. But he certainly intended to find out.

DEVON COULDN'T BELIEVE she'd just said that, or that, for the first time, admitting to a wicked mind wasn't just wishful thinking. Ever since Sydney had driven her home after seeing Cassie's plane off, Devon had been thinking things and saying things she never had before. Must be the underwear.

Sydney had gifted her friend with a beautiful matching bra and panty set in denim blue, satiny and skimpy enough to be decadent but casual in line and generous in comfort so Devon didn't feel like a complete fraud. She had a habit of not wearing underwear at all—more out of pure, self-employed and working-at-home laziness than any sense of heightened sexuality. Syd had insisted Devon wear the sensuous lingerie beneath a pair of Sydney's borrowed jeans, a size smaller than Devon usually wore, and her blouse—unbuttoned and tied with a sassy knot just above her waistline. At least her habit of hammering out plot problems while walking on the treadmill had paid off with a body slim enough to wear the style well, despite her particularly unappeasable cravings for Doritos and ice-cream sundaes.

Still, Devon realized the bulk of her increasingly bold sensuality had nothing to do with her clothes and everything to do with Jake. Taller than she was by a good foot, he'd intimidated the hell out of her when they'd met, first with his size and natural authority and then with his potent blend of masculinity and sweet-natured humility—a trait she'd rarely found in the cops she'd worked with when researching her books.

She suspected Jake was a man of many layers. And damn if she didn't want to peel those layers away, starting with his polo shirt and worn-in-all-the-right-places jeans.

He was right. She did have a wicked mind.

Suddenly, the air around her thickened with moist heat—and not simply because she stood mere inches away from him. The air conditioner had apparently died along with the elevators and lights. In Florida, even in late spring, no coolant or circulation meant incredibly fast jumps in temperature, particularly inside old, musty buildings.

Devon tugged her blouse just below her neckline, creating a quick billow of air.

"It's only going to get hotter if we stay up here," he said.

She couldn't resist raising an eyebrow. "Is it now?"

"Okay, cut that out. Let me rescue you first, then you can flirt. Please." He stood straighter and thrust his hands on his hips. "I order you to resume flirting immediately after I've found the stairwell and have led you to safety."

She suppressed a grin and hooked her thumb to her

right. "The stairs are behind you. Right below that big, red sign that says exit."

"Perfect," he answered, not the least chagrined that he'd missed something so obvious. He stepped across and gave the door a push. The hinges creaked, but the door barely moved. He put his massive shoulder into his second attempt and, though the door protested, it complied with his order to open.

"My lady," he said with a gallant sweep of his hand.

"Very chivalrous of you," she said as she sauntered past. "Want to carry my books, too?"

He smiled but shook his head. "Not when they are in your purse. The leather clashes with my belt. Sorry."

Devon laughed and started down, amazed that they felt so comfortable around each other to tease and banter. They had known each other for seven weeks, but exchanging a few words of introduction and asking a barrage of questions about the course material didn't exactly qualify as getting to know one another. That would happen over dinner. Then and only then would Devon decide if she would hit Detective Tanner with her most shocking proposition to date.

Not so surprisingly, Devon hadn't thought about her book deal until this instant. Her morning had been overrun with emotions. First, sadness over Cassie leaving, then giddy excitement over transforming herself into a sexier, freer Devon Michaels. Cassie had insisted on lending her aunt the sleek, dangly earrings she wore after Sydney squealed about their plan during check-in. Knowing Cassie wholeheartedly approved of her plan to socialize more—all she'd admit to her underage niece—imbued Devon with even more self-confidence.

Today, Devon was no longer afraid of her impulses or her femininity. She'd explore them without regret, without the logic that often directed her to the safety of her loneliness. She'd devote herself entirely to exploring her sexuality—not for the book, but for herself.

And she was fairly certain Jake wouldn't mind.

But lying to him or in any way deceiving him about the motivation behind her newfound interest in her sexuality wasn't an option. Devon may have conquered the world of fiction, but she was a terrible liar. Besides, she liked Jake. She wouldn't risk allowing misconceptions to ruin what could be a carefree, once-in-a-lifetime opportunity. She needed him to teach her about eroticism, about seduction, about sensuality. Yes, to improve her writing...but also to improve her soul.

A little heavy for first-date conversation, but she'd tell him—once she knew she could completely trust him and that he wouldn't think her entirely insane.

"Hold up, Devon. I should walk in front of you. Those emergency lights aren't doing much damage in this stairwell."

He was right. Two or three of the beams, located on

each landing after a dozen or so stairs, seemed to be either very dim or not working at all. They'd hit a particularly dark section, and even though Devon enjoyed the lack of light—the need to feel around with her hands, the thrill of the unknown—she stopped and waited for him to move around her.

She felt his hands on her back, gentle, tentative, before his entire body brushed around hers. He jogged down two or three steps and instructed her to brace her hands on his shoulders.

She hesitated. He'd given her an extremely good reason to touch him, experience the massive power she suspected moved beneath his skin in the hardened sinews of his muscles, but she was too much a creature of habit—too used to not touching and not being touched—to jump in with both feet.

"I'll guide us," he assured her, his voice reasonable and soft.

She lowered her palms onto his shoulders, inhaling as the rock-hard feel of him sent an earthquake of sensation from her fingers to her brain. Guidance. That's what she needed. A nudge in the right direction, a compass to point her toward the sensuality she'd never allowed herself to discover while she raised her sister's daughter and nurtured her career. She tightened her hold on his corded muscles, imagining for an instant how delicious touching him harder and deeper could be.

"I'm counting on you guiding us, Jake. I'm counting on that more than you know."

3

THEY ARRIVED at the bottom of the stairs safely, but the minute Jake tore open the door at the bottom, torrential sheets of rain whipped past the threshold. Lightning slashed against the dark afternoon sky, imbuing the air with electric fire that prickled Devon's skin. God, she hated lightning, particularly when it made her squeal like a schoolgirl.

Jake slammed the door shut and shook his head. Rainwater splashed toward her.

"You're soaked!"

Jake wiped the skin on his arms. "Pretty much. There's no awning out there, not that it would help in this weather. Give me your keys," he volunteered, holding out his hand. "I'll drive your car up real close. You won't get that wet."

"You're not going out in this monsoon! This is Florida, right? If you don't like the rainy weather, you wait ten minutes. It'll die down. Let's just stay here."

And as a native Floridian, Devon also knew that while most afternoon thunderstorms lasted less than an hour, this was not a typical downpour. The sky was different—the color, the clouds, the weight of the atmosphere. Eventually, the lightning would stop, but the rain would likely continue until nightfall—leaving them trapped, alone, him damp and her sweaty, in a hot, dusty stairwell with hardly any light and nowhere to sit except the cramped stairs.

Not exactly the worst situation they could be in, considering her desire to get to know Jake better.

"It's just rain," Jake insisted.

"Rain and lightning. You know it's not safe running across a wide-open space like the parking lot, particularly with my metal keys in your hand. Unless you want to find out what Ben Franklin's kite felt like. I guess I'm a big wimp about lightning, but we all have our phobias, right?"

Jake didn't respond, and though Devon's eyes had sufficiently adjusted to the lack of light, she couldn't read his expression.

Until he walked closer.

Raindrops glistened on the tanned skin of his face, clung to lashes she realized were short but thick, a perfect dark frame for eyes the color of fine liquor in a cut-crystal glass. Even in the dimness, she could see flecks of amber swimming in the topaz, faceted with the colors of the earth. And in those eyes she saw a storm of uncertainty swirling around a torrent even she, inexperienced as she was, recognized as desire.

Devon swallowed deeply. Losing herself in those eyes or, better yet, finding herself reflected within them proved a powerful draw. She couldn't—wouldn't—stop herself from raising her hand to his cheek, even if in the guise of wiping moisture off his skin.

"Anyone with an ounce of sense is wary of lightning. What else are you afraid of?" Jake asked.

Tracing his jawline, Devon didn't speak, entranced by the sensation of his smooth flesh roughened to a sensual texture by the fine grit of his five o'clock shadow—invisible to the eye but indisputable to the touch. She wanted to feel his lips. Were they soft? Moist? He'd asked about her fears at the precise moment she considered facing her deepest one head-on.

Kissing him. Kissing him and not being able to stop.

"Only the lightning," she answered.

Which wasn't far from the truth. No doubt his kiss would be as high voltage as the storm, and perhaps as potentially searing. She inched her touch to his temple, the wet, silky strands of his hair brushing her fingertips. A surge of pure electric need shot through her arm, dispersing an array of tiny, hot pinpoints to her breasts, her belly and below.

Yes, she was afraid of the lightning, present in the form of the concentrated fire of desire. But despite her fear, she moved closer.

When he grinned, his skin tautened beneath her palm. "You must be afraid of more than just lightning."

"Must I?" She let her purse drop beside her, then lowered her hand to his and tugged him to sit on the stairwell. With his huge body, they barely fit, forcing her to sit flush against his thigh. She hoped he couldn't see her triumphant grin in the near darkness. "Tell me one of your phobias first, and then maybe I'll dig out another one for you."

"I don't scare easy," he answered, shifting slightly. The front of his jeans had been soaked, along with his shirt. She figured he was growing more and more uncomfortable in the escalating heat. Or at least, she hoped he was.

"Oh, of course, I forgot." She leaned back on her elbows. "You're a big, bad cop, not afraid of anything. And here I thought you were different."

He mirrored her casual pose, and for a moment she imagined they were lying in a satin-sheeted bed exchanging sexy repartee rather than sharing cloaked innuendoes on a gritty concrete staircase. "Different? From whom? Other men?"

"Other cops." And other men, but she didn't have more than her instincts to support that argument. "I've met my share of your colleagues researching books, attending classes like yours, at the occasional book signing where they delight in telling me that the underworld isn't as glamorous or adventurous as I make it out to be in my books, that I don't know about true life—which is fine since I don't write true life. Always a lot of bravado, loads of self-confidence, the occasional touch of arrogance in some...in most."

"Those qualities in a cop aren't so bad when he's facing death or serious injury on a regular basis. And, for the record, most female cops are just as cocky."

"I know," she assured him. "And don't for one

minute think I don't consider you a prime example of a cocky cop."

"You said I was different—or that you thought I was."

"I did—I do. Trouble is, I can't pinpoint what that difference is."

Pushing away any lingering hesitation, Devon reached out and traced the shape of his shoulder down to his biceps. Once she'd touched him on the way down the stairs, she found she couldn't stop. Touching him became intrinsic, natural...innocent, even though she suspected the concept of innocence and sexy Jake Tanner could never coexist. Trapped so close, she inhaled the subtle scent of his cologne—a mixture of sandalwood and spice, smoothed by a hint of vanilla. A powerful elixir. A perfect match for the man.

"Then you'll just have to get to know me better," he said.

"That's the idea."

He shifted again, growling a little as he moved. "Damn, it's hot in here."

"It doesn't help that you're all sticky and wet. You can take your shirt off. I won't be offended."

Jake laughed. "My jeans, too?"

"Well, if you must," she said, trembling inside while she pretended his stripping down to his boxers would be a tremendous imposition on her sensibilities. "I'm sure I can manage to keep from fainting."

He shifted, pulling his shirttail out of his waistband. "I'll bet you say that to all the guys."

"There aren't any guys in my life, Jake. Haven't been for a long time."

Her voice, a clear yet private whisper, seemed to echo all the way up the stairwell. Devon couldn't believe she'd admitted something so personal, but it was the truth—and he deserved to know, particularly under the circumstances. Devon could change her clothes, her hair, her makeup—but she couldn't change who she was now or who she'd been for the past seventeen years. Sooner or later, her motives and her inexperience would color whatever transpired between them. And while she wasn't ready to come completely clean about her reasons for pursuing him, she could at least lay the groundwork.

"Because you spend all your time writing?" Jake guessed.

Perceptive, this cop with the humble-pie smile. "Mainly. But even before my first contract, something always managed to waylay my social life. When I was fifteen, my sister had a baby. She was only seventeen, but my mother didn't believe in adoption. She insisted, thankfully, that we keep Cassie. A couple of months after her birth, Darcy, my sister, turned eighteen and got an offer to sing professionally—her big break, a chance of a lifetime. So Mom and I raised Cassie. Well, I raised her. Mom had serious diabetes and died when Cassie was about five years old. She's been my number-one priority for a long time, just above my career and *way* above dating."

"Can't blame you. Not after you saw what dating did to your sister...and, indirectly, to your niece."

God, he understood! He'd probably seen more than his share of motherless children and foster-care throwaways. The cops she'd met always had a healthy respect for responsible parenting. And if Devon had been anything, she'd been a damned good mother, even if she hadn't given birth.

She bit her lip, wondering how much more she could tell him, how much she needed to, how much he would understand. When she tried to form the words to explain about the book contract and her financial independence and her private need to have an affair but no long-term relationship, she knew she'd sound like a heartless user—as if she'd only flirted with him to gain the knowledge she needed to make money, further her career, have some fun and nothing more.

But that wasn't the whole truth. She'd been fighting her attraction to Jake since the first moment she'd walked into the classroom, since the first night his image had slid into her dreams and stirred her into an orgasmic frenzy that left her sheets wet with sweat and her body primed for the real deal. Now she had the chance to make that dream real. For herself. For him.

And for the book.

No matter how she tried, the facts wouldn't go away.

"Cassie left this morning to join Darcy in Europe," she told him. "I now have the rare opportunity to do some serious reevaluating of my life."

"Leaving you *alone* to do some reevaluating." He chuckled, but the sound, deep and brief, lacked any humor. "I know the feeling. I admitted to the class that I was off work this week, but I didn't tell you all why."

Jake stared at the dusty beam from the emergency light mounted above them on the first landing. Even in the dim glow, the man had a magnificent profile—high forehead, defined cheeks and a rugged, square jaw. The slight bump on his nose, more than likely from a break, offset his perfection, making him human, real.

"You mean your suspension?"

Her knowledge turned his head, putting his lips only inches from hers and forcing her to take in both halves of his devastatingly handsome face, up close and personal.

"How did you know about that?" he asked.

She shrugged. "What other reason would you have for being home all week, digging into cold cases instead of working an investigation? I read in the paper that an undercover detective had been suspended for allegedly roughing up a suspect in a domestic violence case, but that the force was withholding his name pending an investigation. That's you, isn't it?"

Jake nodded, his gaze wandering toward the light. "Guilty, as charged."

"Should that scare me?"

She asked the question without a hint of fear, and Jake doubted that Devon Michaels had any true phobias outside her understandable fear of lightning. When he turned and stared into her eyes, the darkness cloaked the blue of her irises but not the curiosity in her expression, her insatiable need to know. He recognized her intensity for one telling reason—he saw the same questions in his gaze each and every time he looked in a mirror. Ever since his run-in with the wife beater. Maybe even before.

Raised in the household of a venerated, small-town minister, Jake had been taught to contain his emotions at the same time he learned to walk. A preacher's son didn't run willy-nilly through the play yard but amused himself in a dignified, controlled manner. A preacher's son didn't shout at the umpire after a bad call but left the Little League playing field with a prayer on his lips for the man's immortal soul. A preacher's son didn't tell when he saw his father shoot out the windows of a brand-new car when the battery went dead or confess that his father had torched a shed filled with donations because a group from the congregation had questioned his ability to distribute the gifts fairly.

What Jake had learned was that anger was an explosive, destructive force. Unleashed, rage could destroy even the heart of a once good and pious man, leaving Jake to wonder about the effects on a world-weary cop.

But he didn't need to worry now. Not here. Not with Devon.

"You don't need to be afraid of me," Jake assured her, determined to push aside his bitter memories and concentrate on this lovely, alluring woman. Still, he did owe her the whole truth. "Not unless you plan on beating the crap out of someone a hundred pounds lighter than you and pregnant with your child."

Devon gasped. "Pregnant?"

Jake swallowed hard. "*Was* pregnant. She lost the baby right there in the living room. Right there on the cold tile floor she'd just finished scrubbing on her hands and knees so he wouldn't lose his temper when he got home from a drinking binge with his buddies. She's lucky to be alive after what that pig put her through."

When Devon slid her hand onto his arm, Jake tensed. Not that the sensation of her velvety fingertips didn't ignite a pleasant heat he wanted to savor, but because he'd revealed some of his anger and allowed a small but potent shard of his rage to sneak through. Jake closed his eyes and concentrated. By the time he tucked the fury inside, she'd stopped rubbing his arm, but hadn't removed her hand.

"Where was your partner?" she asked.

She did indeed know a lot about police procedure. "On his honeymoon. Cade might have been able to stop me. Maybe. I had a rookie watching my back, but he was with the paramedics, and the uniforms hadn't arrived."

"If you're suspended, how come they're letting you continue to teach the community police course?"

Jake shook his head. "Dumb luck. This session is actually sponsored by the union, not the city. They aren't about to put me out of work twice."

"Sweet providence, not dumb luck," Devon countered. "If you'd been forced to resign as my instructor, we wouldn't be here right now." Her eyes flashed with acceptance, even a little humor. "I knew if you were the cop who pounded that guy, you would have had a good reason. Apparently, you did."

"No reason is good enough for losing my cool. I've sworn to uphold the law, not take it into my own hands."

She resumed stroking his arm, creating a light, tingly friction.

"Maybe," she mused. "But losing your cool can be fun under the right circumstances."

Jake's body tensed again, but this time the reaction had nothing to do with tamping down his rage. Since they'd been trapped in the stairwell by the storm, Devon had voiced several veiled references that stoked his blood to a rolling simmer. Her touch threatened to increase the heat to a rapid boil. He'd been cooking alone long enough to know a come-on when he heard one. And coming from Devon, a woman who admitted to little if any experience with men and relationships, he suspected her intentions were exploratory, sexual in nature.

Or at least he hoped.

"Like?" he asked.

"Take off your shirt."

"Why?"

He heard her inhale, then slowly release the breath in a soft whistle. "You want to dissect my request until I change my mind, or do you want a great reason to lose your cool?" she asked.

Jake whipped his shirt over his head and tossed it on the handrail. "Done. Your turn."

"What?"

Jake grinned. He was more than game to play along with her fantasy, but he had no intention of facing the risks or enjoying the payoff alone. Didn't take a rocket scientist to figure out that if you have a beautiful, willing woman trapped with you in a hot, humid stairwell, you don't get undressed by yourself.

God, he needed this. A distraction. A fantasy. The suspension didn't bother him so much, even if this reprimand would be the first in his spotless record with the department. What bothered him, haunted him, was the fact that he'd snapped at all—and so violently. Jake Tanner didn't snap. Jake Tanner didn't lose his iron grip on his emotions, particularly while on the job.

But with Devon, he had a chance to let go in a mutually beneficial, mutually exciting way.

"It's only fair," he reasoned. "Or are you afraid of

being naked with a man? Your list of phobias is growing by the minute."

Devon sat up and tore at her buttons until Jake stilled her hand.

"Let me."

Her fingers trembled, but she nodded, sitting back against the railing and closing her eyes.

"Don't you want to watch?" he challenged.

Her lashes flew open. "Watch?"

He shifted until he could use both hands to slip the first button out of the hole. "I have a feeling that seeing you is going to be a fairly remarkable experience. I thought you might appreciate my...appreciation."

After a brief pause, Devon looked down, then at him. If she was trying to hide the volatile mix of trepidation and expectation in her gaze, she wasn't succeeding. But somehow Jake doubted she'd considered hiding her responses. She didn't seem to possess the necessary guile—and if she did, she'd already made it pretty clear that concealing her needs was a practice she was trying to discontinue. Jake hoped Devon was all she presented herself to be—a woman struggling to discover the depths and nuances of her desire, a woman striving to catch up on what she'd missed.

Because only a woman like that—uncomplicated, honest and curious—would fit into his life right now. Until he knew what he wanted beyond the here and now, until he knew the nature of the increasingly black anger simmering inside him, he couldn't make any promises to anyone.

He lowered his gaze, watching how the flesh on her slim throat undulated when she swallowed deeply. Shadows played on her skin, shimmering with perspiration from the heat and injecting her spiced perfume into the thick air. He undid one button, then the next, with as much care as his large fingers could manage on the delicate blouse. He licked his lips, anticipating the moment he earned a clear, unhampered view of the breasts he'd fantasized about for weeks.

The knot just above the waistband proved an unexpected hindrance.

"You were a Girl Scout, weren't you?" he quipped, tugging at the tightly wound material.

Devon laughed, nearly losing her breath at the surprising break in the tension. "Den mother. I do love a good knot."

He grinned. If his den mother had looked like Devon, he would have stayed in the Scouts into adulthood. "I like a challenge."

In less than ten seconds, he worked the fabric free. He paused, inhaled, then sought and captured her gaze. She nodded in answer to his unspoken question, her stare dipping to his chest, her tongue slowly moistening her lips.

He slipped one hand beneath the blouse just at her shoulder blade and peeled the cotton away. One side, then the other. As he suspected, she was exquisite, from the toned muscles in her shoulders to the petite yet inviting curve of her breasts, barely hidden in a dark-colored scoop of a bra. With one finger, he touched the shallow curve at the base of her throat, then traced a straight line downward, stopping when he met the cool satin holding the cups together.

"Now touch me, Devon."

She'd watched him the entire time, but she blinked as if she'd been concentrating only on the feel of his touch.

"Where?"

"Where do you want to touch me?"

She licked her lips again, her gaze darting to his mouth.

"I think I'll plead the fifth on that one," she answered.

He chuckled, appreciating her all the more. She was beautiful, sexy, willing and had a wicked sense of humor. If not for the darkness inside him, the monsters he carefully kept chained and locked away, he'd allow himself the delusion that he'd found the perfect woman.

But Jake had never been one to permit delusions, at least not for long. Fantasies were fine for the short term—and never at the expense of what was real.

Yet at the moment, the only thing Jake knew to be real was his need to kiss Devon Michaels, to allow her to touch his lips and he hers without touching anything deeper. Like a heart. Or a soul.

"Honey, if you want to kiss me, you don't have to plead at all. I've been wanting to kiss you for a very long time."

"What stopped you?"

He answered by capturing her mouth with his, no reservation, no holding back. The kiss was neither hard nor soft, neither demanding nor punishing. And with no tentative fumbling, he sought her tongue and initiated a rhythm she instantly matched.

She tasted like heaven—a cool mixture of musty rain, the diet soda she'd sipped throughout class and a silky warmth that whet his appetite for more. Much more. With a tentative hold on his control, he smoothed his hands up and down her arms, his eyes flashing open when she slid her hands across his chest and tugged on the tufts of dark hair on his pecs.

The result was both painful and thrilling. She had no way of knowing the sensation rated on Jake's pleasure scale somewhere around number nine, second only to sex. Her nails scraped his skin, creating hot paths of fire that branded him, fired him, compelled him to surrender to his need to feel her breasts in his hands.

Bare. Unswathed by silk or lace.

He pressed the straps of her bra aside, then popped the tiny clasps in the middle of her back. The lingerie melted away in the increasing heat. He couldn't contain a pleasured groan when he buoyed her weighted flesh in his hands.

Soft. Warm. Responsive. The instant he brushed his thumbs over her nipples, they puckered. She clutched his shoulders, and the whimper that escaped their kiss urged him, told him his touch pleasured her, hinted that she wanted more.

Still, he had to hear her desires firsthand.

While he plucked the hot points gently, he lowered his mouth to her neck. "I want to taste you."

Her fingers curled into his hair. "Yes."

Leaning her slightly back, he slid down another step, aligning his mouth with her breasts. One tentative swipe of tongue evoked her sharp intake of breath. Her eyes drifted closed. Her lips were slightly parted.

"Mmm," he murmured. "So sweet."

He tasted her again, this time with a long, lingering swirl, tracing the outer darkness of her pale flesh until her nipple pearled to complete tightness. She arched her back, instinctively, no doubt, urging him to ease her discomfort, pushing him to take more than a quick sample. God, he could pleasure her this way for hours, he thought as he suckled and laved until she cried out his name.

She clutched him, explored him with her hands, as unafraid and enthralled, as hungry and aroused, as he was. Her hands mimicked his tongue, flicking his nipples when he flicked hers, pinching when he pinched, smoothing softly when he finally pulled away.

Her hair, mussed and damp, framed her face. Flushed and swollen, her lips pouted his absence. Her eyes burned with questions he didn't attempt to decipher, desires he knew she didn't fully comprehend. And her breasts... Jake's fantasies had been on the money. Small but round. And responsive. To him.

"Wow," he said, knowing he should weave a better

compliment than that, but his mouth was too thick with sexual hunger to spout poetry, even if she did deserve a sonnet or two for exposing herself so freely.

But now, her fingers inched up her bare rib cage. He could see her fighting the urge to cover herself. He couldn't let that happen, so he grabbed her hands in his.

"Don't. You're perfect. Exactly as I imagined."

A tiny smile curved her mouth. "You've imagined me naked?"

"Yeah. I've also imagined quite a few interesting things we'd do together—naked, of course. Do you mind that I've fantasized about you?"

She thought a moment, nodding slowly before she finally said, "Yes. Definitely."

He found her response difficult to fathom. She was, after all, here with him willingly and had been the one to suggest he remove his shirt. And she hadn't exactly protested when he divested her of her bra. "You do?"

"Uh-huh. And I'm going to mind until you describe your fantasy. In detail. Starting right now."

4

THE DECADENCE of lounging half-naked with a man while he told her his fantasies fired Devon's imagination like no book, no character ever had. Jake sat so close the scent of his body heat, thick with musk and spice, overrode the musty smell of aged concrete and stale air. The taste of his kiss lingered on her lips—coffee from the cup with the fast-food logo and the freshness of the mint he'd popped before the slide show. The moistness lingering on her breasts intensified in the heat. The man sure knew how to use his mouth. For smiling. For kissing. For imparting intense pleasure that could have sent her over the edge if he hadn't stopped when he did.

By closing her eyes, even briefly, Devon easily transformed the dank and shadowed stairwell into a sultan's bedchamber, the stairs they leaned upon a gilded pathway to her lover's elevated bed. And Jake, with his dark skin and firelight eyes, made the perfect sheikh. Mysterious, seductive, dangerous.

She sighed, acknowledging that she'd pulled the scenario straight out of Sydney's last book. As she had suspected, a few moments under this man's spell had her creativity working overtime, with the focus on the erotic, the forbidden—the absolutely essential.

This was her ultimate fantasy. To hear a man tell her about his most secret wants and have her as the object of his most hidden desires. The heart of her womanhood, the place in her soul that contained all that was feminine, surged with seductive power.

"I don't think you want to hear this," Jake said, shifting until he sat up straight. He forced a distance between them that Devon found disconcerting, especially since the view of his back—sleek, muscled and broad—proved just as alluring as his chest, particularly when scored by her nails.

He didn't seem to mind, so she remained reclined, determined to deny her fears and overcome her inexperience. Though her nudity was at least partially hidden by the shadows, tiny prickles of exposure right on the tips of her nipples, nipples still electrified from his intimate kiss, sparked each time he glanced in her direction. Her jeans constricted, making her wonder if the seam running between her legs had a purpose more wicked than holding her pants together. Like torture.

"I do want to hear your fantasy." With a single finger, she touched him, drawing a serpentine shape over the sinuous muscle of his arm. "If you tell me yours, I'll tell you mine."

Her offer seeded a grin that, for once, revealed Jake's straight white teeth. When she'd seen him smile before, his lips rarely parted. As if he was holding back, tapping down his humor.

But the look in his golden eyes, lit by the barest gleam from the emergency lamp above them, testified to a man intrigued by the idea of letting loose, breaking free.

"That's a fair deal, and I'll hold you to it. Unfortunately, my fantasy isn't very creative." He took a deep breath. "We're in the classroom upstairs after everyone has left for the afternoon..."

"Ooh, and a storm rolls in?" she asked.

Jake chuckled at Devon's enthusiasm. "Actually, I didn't fantasize the storm, but it's a great touch. But there was no dark, dirty stairwell. And we had air conditioning."

Devon snickered. "That's not very interesting, now, is it?"

If given the chance, she wouldn't change one thing about their current location. Without the rain and lightning, they wouldn't be trapped. Without the heat, they wouldn't be nearly nude. Without the darkness, she never would have had the nerve to go so far and yet remain so close, so exposed.

"Oh, believe me. What we did together in my fantasy was nothing short of fascinating."

His tone dipped low, into the deep recesses where Devon stored her most forbidden needs. He beckoned her to follow by latching onto a lock of her hair and sliding his fingers down, over her shoulder, curling the soft tress around her nipple until she cooed.

"What is it about long hair on a woman that turns a man on?"

Devon swallowed. She had no idea how to answer his question. Her hair was long because she was normally too wrapped up in a book to expend the effort to have it cut. Normally, she twined it into a quick braid or flipped it into a ponytail.

But today, she'd worn her hair down, at least partially. And when he twirled another long lock between his fingers and stretched it to flick the end back and forth against her other nipple, she was incredibly glad she had.

"Maybe what you're doing..." The tiny, soft swipes of her hair over flesh made tender by his tongue renewed sensations that stole the rest of her thought.

"I'm doing what I fantasized about, only..." He reached around and snatched the tiny clip that held her hair away from her face. As he combed his fingers through her soft braid, she vaguely remembered the argument she had with Sydney over whether to wear her hair braided or completely loose.

They'd comprised, and Devon rejoiced that she'd held her ground. Had she listened to Sydney, Jake would have had no excuse to tangle his hands in her hair, cascading the thick length over her shoulders and down her breasts like a thousand feathery fingertips. He'd have had no reason to press forward and touch his nose to her temple, inhaling the fragrance of her shampoo.

"I love the scent of green apples. Sweet, but with a bite," he said. "Do you bite, Devon?"

"Did I in your fantasy?"

"You might have."

Devon's eyes flashed open, though in the darkness she hadn't realized they'd drifted closed. "You like sex rough?"

Jake paused longer than she expected. "I didn't say that."

A jolt shot up her spine. Before she'd embarked on her course of seduction, she'd suspected Jake to be a demanding lover. His delay in answering confirmed her suspicion.

"You didn't have to say it," Devon responded.

"I can be a gentle lover, Devon. For you, I would be whatever you needed me to be."

He whispered the confession into her ear, close enough for Devon to register the unmistakable sound of complete and total honesty. He would transform himself if she wished him to. He would hold back. Measure his seduction to meet her needs.

He'd probably done the same for countless other women countless other times. Devon squeezed her eyes shut, muttered a curse, then pulled back, reaching over the railing to retrieve her blouse.

She slipped the material between them like a curtain.

"I need you to be honest," she said. "As honest as I'm about to be with you."

"Honest about what? I want you, Devon. I've never felt anything so true in my whole life."

"And I want you just as much. You said you were attracted to me the minute I walked into your classroom." Devon swallowed, needing to make this confession before she hit him with the big one—her book deal. "Did you know I lingered in the hallway for about fifteen whole minutes after only catching a glance of you getting out of your car? I never understood animal attraction until then. Didn't want to understand it. But it's chemical, I guess. You can't fight science."

Jake rewarded her honesty with one of those humble grins of his. She said a quick and silent prayer his magnanimous attitude would last.

"You can fight it," Jake admitted, "but why? We're both single, consenting adults."

"Because I haven't been totally honest with you. I had another reason for staying after class today and inviting you to dinner. And I need to tell you what it is, though I wish I could wait until I've heard the rest of that fantasy."

Jake pursed his lips, as if battling with what she'd said—as if deciding whether or not he wanted to hear any more.

"Come here."

"What? Jake, I..."

"Need to confess something before we turn any fantasies into realities. I get that. But I'm a man who finishes what he starts."

He snagged her blouse, turning the material so she could slip her arms inside. He tugged the sides closed but didn't bother with the buttons. Instead, he guided her into the space between his legs while he moved up a step to allow her room to lean against his chest.

"Relax," he ordered.

Yeah, right. The cadence of his heartbeat knocked against her head. The heat from his flesh seeped straight through her blouse. She braced her elbows on his thighs, not the least surprised that the muscle there proved as hard as the concrete of the stairs. How was she supposed to relax when her entire body thrummed with unfulfilled desire, tempered only by the guilt that she hadn't yet told him about her book deal or his potential part in helping her?

"I said relax, Devon."

"I'm relaxed," she lied.

He snorted, but didn't argue.

"Then close your eyes."

She did as she was told.

"Closed?" he asked, turning her slightly so he could apparently peer at her face.

"Uh-huh."

"Now, you remember that this is a man's fantasy, right? Might be a little rough around the edges."

Devon bit her bottom lip to keep from giggling. If he only knew how rough around the edges some of her fantasies could be, he wouldn't have offered a disclaimer.

"I think I can handle it."

"Well, if I didn't think you could handle it, I wouldn't have fantasized about it, would I?"

She peeked one eye open.

"Okay," he amended, obviously easily ruffled by one skeptical look. She liked that. "If I didn't think you could handle it, I wouldn't *tell* you about this fantasy. It starts with you staying after class to ask me a question."

"About?"

"Arrest procedures."

Devon stilled her tongue, rejecting the natural comment that arrest procedures weren't very sexy. With Jake, they could be more than sexy. She hoped they could be. Would be. Because if he came through for her, she hoped to make his fantasy come true, too.

"You sidled up to me at the desk and wondered if I could show you how it was done. The pat down. The handcuffs."

"What was I wearing?"

"Huh?"

"Come on, Jake. Paint a picture for me, here. I'm a writer—I need details."

She was also a woman who needed to have a grip on the situation.

He paused, and when he answered, he couldn't quite hide his impatience. "You were wearing jeans that were too tight and a white blouse, with just enough buttons undone so I could catch a glimpse of your denim blue bra."

"That's what I'm wearing today," she said.

"Imagine that," he answered, his tone all innocence despite the clear implication that nothing pure or honorable existed in his brain right now—a suspicion immediately verified the minute she opened her eyes and caught the blaze in his intense stare.

She pressed her eyelids tightly together.

"So then what happened?"

He shifted his position, rounding his body closer to hers, creating a cocoon of fiery body heat. "I told you I couldn't arrest anyone if they hadn't done anything wrong. It's the law."

"Cop-out," she said.

"That's what you said in my fantasy, too. Or something like it. So you proceeded to take your clothes off, so I could get you for indecent exposure."

Devon gulped and kept her mouth shut. He was getting to the good part and didn't seem to need any help from her to include enough details to make her body burn. She felt a slight hot pinch between her thighs, and the chafe of her nipples on the fabric of her shirt nearly drove her wild. The moisture of the rain-laden humidity swirled around them, but only intensified the dryness in her mouth.

"You tore your clothes off fast, before I could stop you. Then you went over to the blackboard, spread your hands and feet and asked me to frisk you for hidden weapons."

He didn't say anything for a long time, but his breathing had grown heavier. When he shifted, she felt his erection against the small of her back, straining against the damp, restrictive denim of his jeans.

"Did you find any...weapons?"

"Oh, yeah," he admitted on an exhalation of pure need.

"Did you take them from me?"

"Yeah, then I took you from behind so I could touch you all over and be inside you at the same time. You were so wet, so hot, so tight. You wanted me and I wanted you. Right there. In the classroom with no satin sheets or sweet seduction. Just amazing, remarkable sex. Does that frighten you, Devon?"

Devon didn't move. His words were frank, but his soft tone, coupled with the controlled curve of his body around hers, offset the surprise of hearing his fantasy without romantic words wrapped around it.

This was a man's fantasy, after all. A man she wanted. And though she was the object of his lust, even with her half-undressed and willing, he still managed to hold back.

"I'm not frightened of you, Jake."

"Then tell me your secret. Tell me so we can get on with deciding whose fantasy we try first."

JAKE WAITED, turning his head so he didn't have to watch the light gleam over her perfectly round breasts as they rose and fell with each breath. She'd wanted honesty—and he'd given it to her in spades. He'd never spoken so candidly with a woman, but somehow he sensed Devon needed words that shot straight and true.

"I need you to teach me about sex—well, not sex, exactly. I do know about the mechanics. Firsthand," she said pointedly.

Jake nodded. She wasn't a virgin. *Got it.*

She continued, "But I need to know what makes an encounter between a man and a woman truly erotic, unforgettable. And not just for my own personal pleasure, though I'm having a hard time remembering any other reason right about now."

Jake grinned. Devon wore her desire so plainly, her confession seemed unnecessary. He couldn't imagine anything she could tell him that would diminish his need to be inside her, feel if she was as wet and tight as she was in his daydream.

"What other reason?"

"A book."

His body stiffened. "Excuse me?"

"I've been contracted to write an erotic thriller, but I'm having a little trouble with the erotic part. I don't have the experience. I don't know what it means to want someone...or at least, I didn't. Today alone has provided a wealth of knowledge, feelings I can't yet put into words, but they're there, on the tip of my tongue." She turned and leaned on his thigh. "I need you to show me more."

Jake frowned, despite the openly desperate, art-lessly libidinous look in her eyes. Devon Michaels managed to combine logic and keen sophistication with a wild need for passion that tugged at the core of his wants and desires.

"So you want me because of a book deal?" He didn't know how he felt about that just yet, so the words came out sounding completely calm and mildly curious.

"No, I wanted you before I realized my book deal might not pan out. But now I have a perfect excuse to follow through. Do some hands-on research."

"Why do you need an excuse?"

She laughed and rolled her eyes. "If you knew me better, you wouldn't have to ask. I *always* need a reason for doing anything outside my normal routine."

Jake could identify with that mode of operation since in his life outside work he pretty much did the same thing. His partner, Cade, constantly ragged at him to loosen up, take more chances. Be spontaneous. Of course, this came from a man who'd met and married a woman within a few weeks' time. If Cade could see him now, he'd be proud as punch.

"I guess that's the trouble," Jake concluded. "I don't know you better. What do you say we go have that dinner? We could order out from my place."

"Then you'll do it? You'll be my tutor?"

Jake grabbed her hands, pulling her up with him as he stood. "I haven't decided yet." He made a fumbling attempt at buttoning the top button of her blouse, but she smiled and quickly took over. She didn't seem concerned with the loss of her bra, so he snagged the forgotten lingerie off the stairwell and stuffed it in his back pocket.

As he reached for the door, Devon grabbed his arm at the wrist. Her eyes flashed with uncertainty, but she took a deep breath and for the second time that day pushed difficult words out of her mouth.

"I have to be clear, Jake. I'm not looking for a relationship—I mean, nothing serious. Wedding rings and children and arguing over whose family we spend Christmas with are not in my immediate future."

Jake laid his palm over her hand, impressed by her independence, her honesty. "An offer I can't refuse, huh? What guy could say no to a no-strings-attached sexfest?"

Devon's frown quivered with exasperation, leading him to believe she'd heard the facetious bite in his voice. *Good.* Jake had his share of faults and bad habits, some worse than others—some that truly scared him—but no one in his life would ever accuse Jake Tanner of being shallow.

"That's not it. I'm on my own for the first time in my life. This is all very exciting to me. I don't want any misunderstandings between us. I like you, Jake. Obviously," she said wryly, glancing over her shoulder at the stairwell. "I like you a lot."

Jake kissed her hand. "Got it. No strings."

He opened the exit door, throwing rainstorm-dimmed sunlight into the dark space as she grabbed her purse.

"The rain has let up. You can follow me home."

She bit her lip, and Jake could see a flash of regret in her eyes.

"Unless you want to go to a restaurant? We could do that, too."

"No, that's not what I was thinking about. I was hoping to catch a ride on that motorcycle of yours."

Jake's chest swelled with a mix of pride and excitement. He'd had lots of women express a desire to ride with him on his bike, but he'd never offered. Never wanted to. But he'd had a pretty vivid fantasy of riding with Devon—one just as hot as his scenario in the classroom. He never figured her for the type.

Apparently, he'd figured wrong.

"Ever ride a bike before?"

She shook her head.

"Then you'll need educating there, too. Boy, for a rich author, you don't know much."

He held the door open for her and swallowed a smirk when she met his gibe with a quick flash of tongue.

"My sister is rich. I'm just getting by, like everyone else. I haven't earned that big advance yet."

Jake's first impulse was to doubt her claim, but somehow he had trouble believing Devon Michaels lied or exaggerated. She'd already made one shocking confession—about her book deal—and he still didn't know how he felt about it or whether the revelation colored his deeply rooted desire to act out his fantasy—a fantasy he'd been certain would shock her. She'd barely raised an eyebrow.

And she claimed to need education in the sex department? Jake doubted she had any idea how much she would learn if she'd listen to her instincts. Though he could use a refresher course himself in that subject, he couldn't think of a better study partner than the woman who slipped her hand into his as they dashed into the rain.

5

DEVON HAD NEVER been so wet in her entire life. Her jeans, saturated and, if possible, tighter, adhered to her legs as if glued. Her hair dripped rivulets down her back, and when she pulled the strands into a ponytail and squeezed, a full ounce of water pooled at her feet. She'd long ago wiped away any vestiges of makeup or mascara. But looking over the balcony outside Jake's third-floor apartment on Tampa's south side, she felt a light drizzle misting from the stubborn gray clouds fogging the night sky. She couldn't resist tipping her face into the moisture.

Wet was good. Wet with Jake was very, very good.

For as long as she could remember, Devon had been fearful of rainstorms. She'd been the one to watch from the window while Darcy splashed in the puddles without shoes or even an umbrella. She remembered consoling herself with snide guesses that her sister would come down with a nasty case of ringworm or possibly pneumonia, as Mother always predicted, from dancing in the cloudy pools of rain and limestone that formed in the unpaved roadway outside their double-wide trailer.

But tonight, riding through the rain with her arms

locked around Jake's waist and her face buried against his back, their increasing speed turning the soft shower into shards of ice, she'd never felt so invincible. So powerful. So healthy and alive and free.

A flash of silent lightning in the distance reminded Devon that her time with Jake was little more than an illusion. Her fear of storms remained deeply rooted, even if she'd managed to push the terror aside for a little while.

Always a careful plotter, Devon had decided her dalliance with Jake could last one week, two at the most. She had a book to write, a life to lead. A long-term relationship could never fit into her long-ignored goals. She wanted to feel the pressure of true independence, act with selfish desire above all else—for the first time in her life. Devon knew herself well enough to guess that if she allowed herself too much time with Jake, she'd start to care—more than she already did after only one evening. And if she cared, she'd do with him what she'd done with every other person in her life from her mother to Cassie to Darcy to Sydney. Take care of them. Nurture them. Put their needs and desires above her own.

If she kept their affair brief, her needs and desires and Jake's could remain one and the same.

Pleasure.

She snuggled close to the wall and waited beneath the pink light outside Jake's apartment, loath to imagine what she looked like with her hair wet and wind-blown and her blouse completely transparent. Not that Jake would consider that part unattractive, she imagined. She'd left the stairwell without retrieving her bra and had nearly asked to go back until she spied a blue satin strap sticking out of his pocket.

Jake wanted her braless—and she enjoyed the thrill of giving him what he wanted. She also enjoyed the thrill of riding behind him with her unbound breasts pressed against him, softness to hardness. While they flew down a lightly used stretch of the interstate, the glow of the traffic lamps no more than a tangerine blur, she'd wondered what riding naked would feel like, particularly with her thighs clinging to his.

But first things first.

Devon glanced at her bare wrist. Sydney had insisted Devon abandon her watch today for the symbolic power alone. She had no one to go home to, no one who expected her. She had all the time in the world to explore a new life.

But hours must have passed since they'd called in their dinner order and hit the open road, arranging for the meal to be delivered to a neighbor so they could ride as long as they wanted. Her stomach growled. They'd made a quick stop at a gas station for refueling and bathroom breaks, but otherwise they'd ridden with no purpose but to feel the speed swallow them whole and feel each other in the process.

Devon hadn't thought once about the book deal— well, no, that wasn't entirely true. Barely five minutes into the ride, she'd decided that her heroine's love interest would ride a motorcycle. But once she'd filed that character clue away, she embraced the new experience with a mindless focus on her senses. She'd done something wild, something slightly dangerous, something totally outside her comfort zone. Outside her very neat, very controlled universe. And she wanted more.

Jake still hadn't agreed to her proposition, but they hadn't discussed the book deal or his part in her education since they'd left the stairwell. He'd given her no indication that he wouldn't accept her offer, except for his silence on the subject, which did concern her. Maybe she needed to sweeten the deal.

She furrowed her brow, wondering what she could possibly contribute that would appeal to Jake more than a no-strings, sex-based affair where she was ready, willing and able to try nearly anything once. Of course, she hadn't exactly said all that yet, but just a few hours in his company convinced her Jake was a man she could trust, a man who could keep secrets and be discreet.

He had to say yes.

She didn't know all that many men, but she was fairly certain her proposition, when rated on the list of things men desire, might rank slightly below being a quarterback in the Superbowl or owning the fastest, sleekest car ever built. But then again, Jake had always seemed a bit different. Maybe his desires ran deeper—or darker, as he'd hinted. A concentrated electric surge shot from between her thighs the moment she recalled his rough-and-ready classroom fantasy and the basic, unpoetic language he'd used to describe what he'd do with her. How and where he'd touch her. Arouse her. And how she'd react. She closed her eyes and let the image form again. The intimate pulsing between her legs intensified to the point where she knew she could orgasm right there if Jake so much as brushed his hand against her.

Luckily, she managed to pull herself together before he came out of the apartment next door with a large paper bag steaming with the scents of garlic and fine Romano cheese.

"It's still hot?" she asked, watching how he gingerly balanced the bag on his hip while he took out his keys and worked the lock.

"Mrs. Galucci tucked it in her oven for us. She likes me."

He rewarded her with one of those humble half grins of his, and Devon trembled with need. God, the man was lethal. And he probably had no idea—at least, not in the sense she meant. She couldn't forget the pain in his eyes when he'd told her about his suspension for beating up a man he was supposed to arrest. His action weighed heavily on him, which made her admire him all the more.

"What's not to like about you?" she asked.

His smile faded. "You don't really want to know the answer to that, do you?"

"I want to know everything about you," she replied, aware that her honest answer probably wasn't what he wanted to hear. Jake may have offered his sexual secrets easily, but naive or not, Devon understood human nature well enough to recognize a man who held on tightly to his personal mysteries, perhaps even cloaking them from himself.

He opened the door and motioned her to enter first. "I wouldn't want to bore you."

She laughed, shaking her head while he flipped on the light. "You don't scare easily, and I don't bore easily."

"I'll bet you don't."

Not surprising, the state of his apartment lingered between neat and lived-in. He had a wall of black iron shelves lined with books and compact discs and videos, but a quick, close glance revealed that they needed a good dusting. His carpet was worn in all the typical spots but had been vacuumed so recently that the track marks from the machine were still visible. The space, decorated in warm, earthy browns and blacks and dark reds, sported animal-print pillows in zebra and leopard, with African artifact replicas placed strategically around the room.

This surprised her. That Jake would have a neat apartment was expected, but the decorator touches didn't seem his speed.

"Nice place," she remarked, drawn to a fascinating print in his dining area featuring a herd of charging elephants.

"My sister did the decorating, if you're wondering."

"I was. I didn't know you had a sister."

Jake attempted to look annoyed at the mention of his sibling, but Devon recognized the glow of affection when she saw it. In her world, balanced doses of annoyance and affection were the emotions best associated with sisters.

"Kat's a trip. She's a journalist—this week," he said. "Freelance magazine stuff, mostly, although she also dabbles in television from time to time."

"Does she live in Tampa?"

"Los Angeles. But Kat is the type to show up at anytime or anyplace, without fanfare or announcement, and just expect you to take her in. Last time she hit town, she decided to repay my hospitality by decorating the place in pre-Columbian jungle safari."

Devon watched his stare glide around the room, as if he hadn't noticed the decor for quite some time.

"Well, I like it," she concluded. "The leopard prints, the dark, earthy colors. Very Jake Tanner, I think. Maybe your sister knows you better than you think." Then she added, "And I get the idea that the concept of anyone knowing you too well bothers you."

Jake set the bag on the kitchen counter and eyed her narrowly from the pass-through between his small cooking area and a glass dining-room table flanked by two wrought-iron chairs and set with candles that had obviously never been lit.

He opened his mouth to respond, then closed it with a growl she wasn't sure she was supposed to hear. By the time he spoke, his tone was one of utter nonchalance.

"You should change out of those wet clothes while I put out some plates and stuff. My bedroom is the last door. Grab anything to wear."

Devon slid around the table and leaned toward him on the bar. "What if I don't want to wear anything?"

Jake's grin was small but potent—and this time his growl reverberated loud enough so his frustration was more than obvious.

"Fine with me." He popped open the cardboard top of the penne carbonara he'd ordered, then lifted the container so the steam would float toward her. "But if you arouse my other appetites too soon, you won't get a bite of this for several hours."

The spicy scents of strong red pepper, sweet tomato, tangy smoked prosciutto and rich cheeses made her nostrils flair and her eyelids flutter. Her stomach responded with a grumble louder than Jake's, only the sound wasn't very sexy coming from her. Food first. She could flirt and eat at the same time, she was certain. She disappeared down the hall, popping buttons as she walked.

JAKE GROANED with relief when he heard the door to his bedroom close. He needed a minute to regroup. A minute? An hour! Days, even. But he didn't have days. He needed a plan right here, right now. The woman had him knotted tight, and if he didn't pull himself together and focus, he might follow her straight into his bedroom and do the getting-to-know-you part in a horizontal position.

And while he was damned certain she wouldn't protest, Jake held fast to the last vestiges of common sense and romantic finesse and determined they should at least eat and chat first.

He covered the pasta and headed for the refrigerator, needing the cool blast of air that nearly froze his wet clothes while he stood there with the door open. He took his time choosing from the two bottles of wine on the top rack. One was a fruity white dessert wine his sister brought last time she dropped in, the other a half-full green glass jug of Chianti Mrs. Galucci sent over when she decided it gave her heartburn. Nothing fancy or imported. They'd have to make do.

He grabbed the Chianti, fairly certain Devon wouldn't be a wine snob any more than she was a snob about anything else. The information he'd read on her didn't say much about her childhood or her upbringing, but humble beginnings were mentioned more than once. He realized he probably would have found out more if he had done a little research on her sister, but Jake suspected Darcy's experience and Devon's were not identical, even if they had been raised in the same household.

He pulled out plates and wineglasses, blowing away the dust before rinsing them thoroughly and giving them a quick dry. He set out silverware and hunted down the zebra-striped placemats and napkins he'd stashed in a drawer after getting dizzy from the wild pattern one morning while chomping his Cheerios. They weren't so bad once he lit the half dozen mismatched candles Kat had artfully arranged in the center of the table.

He scooped out large portions of salad, tossed garlic bread in a basket and filled the wineglasses. He was damned impressed when he stepped back to survey the picture.

Very romantic. Very classy.

Damn, he wasn't so bad at this. Seduction was simple, really. Simple.

As in, keep it simple, stupid. The KISS principle.

Aha!

Jake grinned. Devon's request that he tutor her in the art of lovemaking had thrown him for a loop. Not because he didn't have the knowledge, of course, but because he wasn't sure how he should go about presenting the course material to a woman who boiled his blood to the point where it fried the circuits in his brain. But now? He had a solid idea. One he could use.

"Wow, that's some spread."

Devon came around the corner wearing his old rookie T-shirt, dark blue and nearly threadbare but sinfully soft after twelve years of washings and fabric softener. He'd left it on the corner of the bed, intending to wear it to sleep in as he had the night before...and the night before that. But as he watched the supple cotton mold against Devon's curves, he knew he'd never wear the shirt again without experiencing an instantaneous hard-on.

He swallowed, forcing moisture into his mouth. "I have other shirts that are clean."

She lifted the sleeve and gave it a sniff. "Smells clean to me. Smells like you."

She snagged a wineglass and sipped, smiling as she swallowed. "Why don't you go change and I'll put on some music?" She plucked a green olive off a salad plate and popped it in her mouth. "But hurry. I'm starving."

He was pretty damned hungry himself and felt certain Devon knew exactly what his appetite truly craved. When she shuffled across his fake lion-pelt rug and reached up to grab a CD from a top shelf, he caught the ivory gleam of bare bottom—very round, very smooth.

She was wearing nothing beneath his T-shirt, and when she glanced over her shoulder before focusing her attention on the liner notes, he knew without a doubt she'd wanted to make sure he knew it.

Inexperienced, his ass. Maybe Devon didn't have a long line of lovers to account for her sexual knowledge, but the woman's instincts were perfectly honed. What the hell could he teach her?

He mulled the question over as he changed into a pair of worn sweatpants and a plain gray T-shirt. He used his fingers to comb his hair, grimacing when he noticed how rough his cheeks were. After a quick pass with his electric razor and a swig of mouthwash that wouldn't last very long with all that garlic, Jake opened his bedroom door to the sound of...singing.

Devon sings?

Jake stopped at the doorway. She was playing a CD he hadn't heard in a long time—if ever. More than likely one of the many Kat had given him after her stint as a music critic ended. He didn't know the artist, but the rhythm was definitely slow and sultry. A rock-and-roll ballad about bittersweet love.

He didn't know that because of the lyrics. He'd barely heard two measures. No, he knew from the timbre of Devon's voice. Deep, dulcet tones that reached into her heart and tugged the sounds free.

Devon could sing.

He shouldn't have been surprised. Her sister had enough talent to pack stadiums. But the fact that Devon felt free enough to sing around him—that shocked him. Whenever he caught Kat singing in the shower or to the radio in her car, she protested loudly, as if he'd intruded into some big secret.

Of course, Kat couldn't hold a tune, and yet she probably still fancied a future as a rock star. Devon, on the other hand, knew all about that lifestyle and had obviously made a conscious choice to remain out of the limelight.

He walked quietly down the hall, stunned when he peeked around the corner and caught her swaying softly during the instrumental interlude, her back to him. Before he thought too long about his two left feet, he slid behind her and slipped his arms around her waist, careful not to jostle her drink.

She didn't flinch, her body cosseted by the simple rhythms of the music.

"How long were you watching me?" she asked.

"Long enough to realize your sister could have some competition if you decided to take up a music career."

Devon leaned her head on his shoulder. "Not likely."

"You have a beautiful voice," he told her, somewhat disappointed when the lead vocalist started singing and Devon didn't join in.

"Here, in a quiet room, with candlelight and a man I trust." She turned, then tilted her head so she could look into his eyes—so he could gaze into hers. She was lazy with fatigue and wine, and her sapphire irises widened with total openness, complete faith. "I can trust you, Jake, can't I?"

His chest hardened, as if someone had poured instant-drying concrete down his throat. Never in his life had anyone doubted Jake's ability to be trustworthy. He could have been the damned poster boy for the Boy Scouts, the priesthood and an entire regiment of Canadian Mounties for his well-bred ability to always do the right thing.

Until last week. Until he realized most of the perps he'd collared got back on the street one way or another. Until he'd become a cop who could no longer turn off the bloody images of man's inhumanity to man.

Funny, but while gazing into Devon's soulful stare, he couldn't bring one of those gory pictures to mind. Not that he tried very hard. Especially not after she licked her wine-stained lips with a slow, wet tongue.

"I won't reveal your secrets," he assured her. "Not even that you sing better than your sister."

She chuckled with an adorable snort. "You can tell that one. No one will believe you."

"Suppose I claimed you were the sexiest woman I'd ever met?"

Her snort turned into a cough as she pulled away, grabbing his hand and leading him toward the table. "You'd have no one to dispute or agree one way or another, I'm afraid."

"You keep saying that," Jake said, helping her slide into a chair before settling into his own, "but I'm having a really hard time believing you're so inexperienced."

She grabbed her fork, her eyes widening as she stabbed a chunk of tomato off the top of her salad. "Why? Because I'm well beyond twenty?"

If Jake had learned one thing from his sister and mother, it was never to inquire about a woman's age, particularly if he already knew the answer. "Your age has nothing to do with it."

The tomato must have been particularly robust, because the minute the red morsel disappeared beyond her lips, her expression changed. As she chewed, the

tension completely melted away, replaced by a bliss-
ful smile that nearly made Jake forget his hunger.

"Wow, this is delicious." She speared another tomato, added a few pieces of romaine and an olive.
"The perfect Italian salad. I wish they'd open a restaurant like this on my side of town."

She devoured her next bite, then the next, eating
with relish and obviously enjoying the flavors and
sensations, even simple ones like fresh garden vege-
tables and Cesare's full-bodied dressing. Jake gener-
ally ignored that part of the meal, spearing a few bites
here and there because the salad came with the entrée.

Devon, however, made the most of every bite.

"See? This is what I mean," Jake closed his eyes and
took a bite, determined to experience the taste explosion for the first time...again.

She halted, her fork halfway to her mouth. "What?
I eat like someone who's eaten before? No kidding."

He chewed slowly, allowing the bold flavors of olive oil, garlic and Parmesan to roll over his tongue.
"No, you eat like you've *never* eaten before. This salad
is stupendous. I order dinner from Cesare's at least
twice a week, but it's been a long time since I remembered just how good it is."

She finished the forkful and stabbed another. "I appreciate the little things, I guess. It's my nature."

"Which makes me wonder how I'm going to teach
you anything about eroticism that you couldn't figure
out on your own."

Her smirk bordered on certifiably cute. "Guess

what, Detective Tanner. Sex isn't so much fun when you do it on your own."

"Really? I'd never guess."

She bit her lip and moved her salad plate aside, then leaned across the table and slid the pasta closer. She filled his plate, then hers, waiting until he took a bite before she spoke again.

"So when's the last time you took matters into your own hands?"

6

ONLY THE QUICKEST reflexes saved Jake from coughing his entire mouthful of food onto his plate. He swallowed most of the pasta whole, forcing it down with a hearty gulp of wine.

"Excuse me?"

She matched his gulp, then raised him one. He refilled her glass, then his. She had the decency to blush a little.

"Would you rather me ask about your last lover?"

"Yes...no! You have a strange concept of dinner conversation, Ms. Michaels." And an incredible capacity to surprise and shock the hell out of him. Yet he knew without a doubt that she'd set out to do neither. She asked whatever question popped into her head, uncomfortable or not, appropriate or not. Probably came from all that experience with interviewing cops. Experience he also had, but that wasn't helping him anticipate her questions one damned bit.

"I thought we were supposed to be getting to know each other better," he said.

"Seems to me I'll know you pretty well if you answer my question," she replied.

She raised her glass in a brief salute, her expression

ever-so-slightly wicked, making him wonder how she managed to retain the quality of innocent wonder that made him want to answer her. He wouldn't, of course. Jake preferred to escape the possible humiliation of revealing how recently he'd indulged in a little solo sexual action. Except, with Devon, he wondered if the secret would be embarrassing. She seemed to have a clear handle on basic human needs—particularly when it came to sex.

Jake narrowed his gaze, wondering how the hell this woman could ask such a question with such total naiveté. She really wanted to know. Really.

"Let's just say I can still remember the last time rather vividly," he answered.

She grinned at the victory, small as it was.

"Yeah. Me, too."

Her confession hung in the candle-scented air for a moment while Jake wondered if he was supposed to respond. But then he remembered he'd decided to keep this interaction with Devon as simple as possible—and jumping into a deep exploration of the topic of self-manipulated sex during dinner didn't seem simple in the least.

"So tell me about your book, this erotic thriller you're having so much trouble with."

Devon ate her pasta with the same enthusiasm as her salad, but she chewed carefully before she spoke. "The thriller part was easy to nail. My cozy mysteries are fun, but I've done nearly fifteen now. Fioranna, my heroine," she explained, unaware that he'd read from cover to cover in one sitting the copy of the book she'd sent, "always arrives after the crime has been committed and has never been a victim herself. My new heroine will be in danger from page one. It's exciting."

"What's her name?"

"Right now? Leah."

"After Princess Leia?" he guessed.

Her grin bloomed. "Are you a *Star Wars* fan?"

He shrugged, unwilling to admit that he'd seen the original movie dozens of times in the theater during the original first-run release. He'd lost count since then, with rereleases and video factored in. Sounded like such a geeky thing, but Jake could still remember the complete awe he'd experienced when those opening credits rolled in time with John Williams's haunting score and the first Star Destroyer had zoomed onto the screen firing hot blue lasers and swallowing up the darkness of space.

"That's so cool," she said. "You know, I can still remember the first time I saw that movie. Darcy had sneaked us in at this old cinema in the mall. She was instantly in love with Han Solo and proceeded to paper our corner of the bedroom with pictures of him. I was, like, seven or eight years old. R2-D2 was more my speed."

Rolling his eyes, Jake surrendered to the memories. He was enjoying this trip into childhood more than he'd expected. "I begged my father to allow me to go. Everyone in my class had already gone, but the Reverend wasn't sure the film would be a good influence on me—all that fantasy and sci-fi stuff. But he gave in, and I'm fairly certain the film set me on my quest to be a cop."

Her eyes widened. "Really? How?"

Jake took a bite of his dinner to avoid giving an immediate answer. Exploring his past, even something as benign as the influence of George Lucas's film on his adult career choices, didn't usually sit well with his live-in-the-now mentality—a process of thinking that he suspected would catch up with him someday.

Perhaps today was a good day. Devon's blue eyes, wide, eager and curious, possessed no hint of judgment, no risk of disapproval. But he'd never go so far as to consider her to be trusting—he'd read her books, seen her interact with others in class. And with him—in the stairwell, on their ride in the rain, while dancing and now at dinner. She protected herself with a healthy arsenal of intelligence and wariness, and yet she didn't seem to let the possibility of being disappointed—or being a disappointment—get in her way of taking a chance.

"I thought the stormtroopers were way cool," he joked.

Her eyes widened. "Stormtroopers! I thought for sure you would want to be Luke Skywalker, off to save the universe."

Shaking his head, Jake finished a last bite of pasta and tore a piece of garlic bread to sop up the sauce. "Sorry, but I was ten years old and totally won over by blasters and Death Stars and shoot-outs in long corridors. It wasn't until later that I decided I should probably be one of the good guys."

She was thoughtful for a moment, swirling a tube of pasta around on her plate. "It's funny, but I'm pretty sure the movie influenced my decision to become a writer. I remember making up a sequel on the bus ride home. Gosh...something to do with Princess Leia finding out that her father—or at least the man she thought was her father—wasn't on Alderaan when the Death Star destroyed it, so she hired Han Solo to help her find him. Darcy loved it so much, she made me write it down so she could show her friends."

Jake thought back to the dozen or so black and white composition books he'd filled with his own tales of adventure and fantasy. He wondered what had ever happened to them. He hadn't thought about his boyish storytelling attempts in years. Snapping back to the moment, he asked, "Do you still have that story?"

Devon finished her wine. "Lord, I hope not! *The Empire Strikes Back*, it wasn't. But I learned the thrill of creating a story other people read and got excited about. Pretty soon I was using my own characters. The rest is history."

"History that is yet to be complete as mystery writer Devon Michaels ventures into the erotic," he said, wanting to bring the topic to the matter at hand. He'd dredged up a relatively simple reminiscence from his past, and now he couldn't seem to stop the flow of memories that followed, no matter how much he tried.

Images of his father shaking his head at Jake's fantastic declaration of wanting to sail to the stars to fight intergalactic battles. The Reverend banning all guns and gunlike toys from the house—except for his own gun, of course. The Reverend railing against science fiction and fantasy during a sermon delivered on Jake's birthday, the birthday on which he didn't receive the retractable light saber he'd wanted more than anything in the world. Instead, he'd gotten a collection of board games bought at a secondhand store, all with biblical themes. From that day forward, his father had taken great pains to remind Jake that he was born to serve the spiritual needs of others, like the Reverend and his father before him.

Jake's needs be damned.

Eventually, Jake had turned away from the father he'd always wanted to please and walked out shortly after high school graduation. He'd enlisted in the marines and then, following his stint as an MP and his training at the police academy, accepted a position in Tampa's undercover force. Even as a rookie, no one ever considered him inexperienced or green. He was too good, too perfect.

But never perfect enough to please his father. Eventually, the pragmatist in him demanded he quit trying. If not for phone calls to his mother and visits with his sister, Jake would have no contact with his family at all. His sister had had the good sense to act the angel with complete precision until her eighteenth birthday, when she'd declared her independence, dyed her hair purple, bought a used Pinto with her squirreled-away allowance and tore out of Smalltown, Florida, without ever looking back. Nowadays neither he nor his sister had anything to do with the Reverend. Jake was always too busy with his work, too wrapped up in a case. Too loath to start the arguments again.

He tried not to consider what his father, retired from the pulpit but no less self-righteous, would say about Jake's suspension. Or his dalliance with a woman who didn't want a wedding ring as a reward for her sexual favors. Luckily, Jake had been making his own decisions about his life for a long, long time. And he'd rarely faced an easier decision than agreeing to help Devon with her fascinating project.

Not that she'd be the only one with something to gain. He'd enjoy a little bit of paradise before he returned to the real world.

Devon clinked her glass on the table and winced at the sound. "Sorry. I think I've had too much to drink."

Jake promptly removed the wine jug from the table. "Can't have that. I demand clear thinking from my students."

"So you've decided to help me?"

There was that naïveté again. Jake couldn't resist a grin. "Was there really any question?"

Devon accepted the subtle compliment with a tiny flush. "But I don't want you to think I'm only interested in you for my book or for the money I'll get if I finally make the sale."

"I would never think that about you."

Her brows shot up. "Why not? You know I wasn't born with money. You know the lifestyle I live is borrowed from my sister and that this book is important to me. It's my chance at real independence, at real success, and I..."

Jake got up from the table, grabbed her hand and pulled her out of her chair and into his arms. The scent of wine lingered on her breath, and the Chianti had stained her lips an alluring shade of burgundy.

"Stop rationalizing, Devon. Give that careful, detail-oriented brain of yours a break. I understand what you want and what you don't want. You've been clear and up-front. You want to explore the attraction between us, but you also want to learn about sex."

"I know about sex," Devon said, her sternness a contrast to the pliant feel of her in his arms. "I told you, I'm not a virgin, Jake. Unfortunately, my lovers have been few, far between and less than memorable, though I can't blame them entirely for not doing things right."

"I would," Jake muttered, quite certain that the sensual woman who'd nearly seduced him to insanity in the stairwell couldn't have been frigid in any part of her lifetime—even prior to her first sexual experience. Scared, sure. Reluctant, most likely. But cold? Not in this century.

She rewarded his claim with a sweet smile. "Thanks. But truth is, I'm a different woman today. And part of that is thanks to you."

"Me? I haven't done anything...much. Not yet."

The sweet smile turned into a full grin, brimming with expectation. "Oh, yes, you have. You've planted a powerful fantasy in my mind. And even before that, you introduced me to a concept I now realize has been missing with any other man. Chemistry."

"You can't teach chemistry. Not this kind, anyway."

"But we've got it, like it or not. I would have gone all the way with you in the stairwell without a second thought, without one ounce of regret. This is powerful stuff between us. Together, we can channel that chemistry—make the most of it. And along the way, an experienced guy like you can teach me the ins and outs of sexual interaction, so to speak."

"I'm certainly up to the challenge," he said wryly, playing her game and garnering a little groan from her.

"You think teaching me about eroticism will be difficult?" she asked, brushing aside the teasing.

"Difficult? That's not the word I'd choose. My challenge is deciding on the approach. How can I possibly teach such an innately sensual woman anything she doesn't already know, deep down, inside that incredibly creative mind?"

Devon swallowed deeply. "But you've figured out a plan, haven't you?"

"I think I have."

"Tell me."

"Baseball."

THE MISCHIEVOUS GLINT in Jake's amber eyes caused a rush of vibrant expectation to swirl straight from Devon's toes to the tips of her breasts, which were pressed against his hard abs. He was so tall, so masculine, so cute when he was being clever.

"Baseball? You're not going to have me running laps or hitting pepper, are you?"

"Hitting pepper? You know baseball?"

"It *is* America's pastime," Devon said, suspecting where he was going with his analogy. Baseball. First base. Second base. Third base. And that all-important home run.

Made her want to order up a hot dog and prepare for a little seventh-inning stretch.

Her unvoiced double entendre caused a girlish giggle to accompany her dance toward the living area. She scooted Jake along with her. The couch was overstuffed and long—perfect. She was quite certain she heard an umpire somewhere yelling, "Play ball!"

"What are you doing?" Jake asked.

She flopped onto the couch and pulled him down beside her.

"Just getting comfortable for a little doubleheader action."

"I thought I was supposed to be calling the plays. You are a fairly bossy woman, you know that?"

"I've been told."

Jake didn't look as dismayed as his tone implied. In fact, his expression was between amused and excited. "We'll have to agree to one big rule. If I'm coaching, I expect to be in charge of the game. I say, you do."

When she realized that she trusted Jake enough to nod instant agreement, a potent shiver shot through her.

"You sure?"

"Positive."

"No quitting? No asking for a trade to another team?"

His insistence on drawing out the baseball analogy caused her to laugh even while an inner voice shouted for the man to shut up and start kissing her, already.

Not that they hadn't kissed. Not that she couldn't immediately relive the sensation of his mouth and tongue exploring and twining with hers just by glancing at his lips. But this time would be different. His eyes sparkled with some unknown piece of information he clearly planned to show her rather than tell her.

She couldn't wait.

"I promise. I'm yours, coach. Do with me what you will."

"Excellent."

But instead of kissing her, Jake rolled off the couch. He snagged the remote control to the stereo and raised the volume, then shut off all the lights in the apartment except for the candles still twinkling from the table and the recessed lighting over the couch, which he dimmed to a warm gold. He disappeared down the hall, returning quickly with something stuffed in his pocket. Then clearing the knickknacks off his coffee table, he sat in front of her.

"So what do I do now? Close my eyes and pucker?" she asked, uneasy with his focused, silent stare.

She expected him to laugh, hoped he would, but his expression darkened with an intensity that knocked the humor right out of her. Jake meant business. She hadn't known him long, but she suspected the man always meant business, no matter what the business was. He appreciated humor and could tease and banter with flair, but at heart, he was a serious man.

A seriously sexy man.

"You told me yourself that you're not some virgin who needs basic lessons in the mechanics, Devon. So we're gonna up the stakes."

Like a magician, he produced a scarf—a dark red bandanna he folded into a three-inch wide band.

"Put it on," he ordered.

"A blindfold?"

He handed her the material in response. She did as he asked, taking a deep breath as the dimly lit room disappeared. She tied the knot extra tight. She was not only going to do everything he instructed, she would kick it up a notch.

"All secure?" he asked.

"Remember that scene in *Star Wars*—"

"Shh. Don't steal my thunder, rookie."

She laughed and pressed her lips together.

"Okay, stand up."

She obeyed with an excited bounce, her hips swaying to the natural rhythms of the music. A thrill shimmied up her bare legs and curled around her bottom. For the briefest second, she'd forgotten she wasn't wearing panties. She wore only his threadbare T-shirt and the blindfold. His scent, previously detectable on the fabric only when she took a direct sniff, wafted to her nostrils unbidden, musky and hot. Without her sight, her other senses surged. The gentle rub of the T-shirt against her erect nipples. The taste of wine lingering on her tongue. The heat of his body inches from hers.

"Now what, coach?"

"Raise your arms over your head. Slowly."

She could hear his voice from below her, his mouth speaking somewhere near her belly. He must be sitting on the coffee table, eyes level with her breasts. Could he see the hardened peaks through the soft material of his shirt? Did it arouse him with the same jolt of electric need as the thought excited her?

She did as he asked, gasping as the hem of the shirt rose with her movement, skimming the tops of her thighs. She heard him move. Was he tilting his head, peeking beneath to watch her swell with want, glisten with need?

She swallowed deeply. *Gosh, wasn't this about base-ball? First base? Kissing?*

The hell with baseball. She wanted him to kiss her, all right. But not on her mouth.

"What are you thinking?" he asked.

She tilted her head. She'd heard him, but the music was so loud, thrumming with bass. Or was that her heart?

"I'm thinking the music is driving me crazy."

In an instant, the volume dipped. "I intend to drive you wild, Devon, but not with loud music."

The coffee table creaked as he shifted. She felt his knees brush hers as he scooted forward, closing the distance between his mouth and her body.

"Keep your arms raised," he directed, "but reach down enough to grasp the material on your shoulders."

She complied, her arms shaking. She wanted to pull, hoist the fabric, fire him with the sight of her nude body so he'd touch her and kiss her and break the atmosphere of anticipation that dried her mouth like an abandoned desert oasis. So she did, lifting the material ever so slightly, and was rewarded with the sound of Jake's appreciative groan.

"You're leading off, Devon," he chastised, still milking the baseball analogy by describing a runner who'd ventured too far off a base.

She licked her lips. "Isn't that the signal you sent me?"

He chuckled. The deep sound traveled across her skin like wildfire.

"Don't anticipate my signals. Just my kiss, my

hands. That, you see, is one of the keys to eroticism. Anticipation. Not knowing, but wondering, guessing. Just like a pitcher who has the other team's winning run on third base."

Swallowing, Devon considered his words.

"Third base? I thought you'd start on first, with kissing. Work your way home."

Jake chuckled. "We already covered first and second base in the stairwell. Child's play, really."

The coffee table creaked. Had he stood? A gentle breeze billowed. From him whipping off his clothes? A tear of foil. A snap of...latex?

This man took his game seriously and had all the right equipment close at hand.

Devon moaned. She'd never felt so on fire, so close to losing control, and he'd hardly touched her. She couldn't see him, could barely feel him, could only imagine the nuclear meltdown she'd experience with his next intimate touch. Or would he taste her with a kiss? When he'd kissed her in the stairwell, he hadn't teased her first. There'd been little by way of buildup, just a quick but gentle claiming that left her breathless and a natural progression to tasting her nipples that had made her want him—all of him.

"The real skill, Devon, is sliding into third. And then stealing home."

Her mind instantly flashed to the fantasy he'd planted earlier. The classroom. Instant nudity. A flood of wet heat. A crash of bodies primed by lust and

An Important Message from the Editors

Dear Reader,

Because you've chosen to read one of our fine romance novels, we'd like to say "thank you!" And, as a special way to thank you, we've selected two more of the books you love so well, plus an exciting Mystery Gift, to send you absolutely FREE!

Please enjoy them with our compliments...

Pam Powers

P.S. And because we value our customers, we've attached something extra inside...

Peel off seal and Place inside...

EDITOR'S FREE GIFT SEAL THANK YOU

How to validate your Editor's
FREE GIFT
"Thank You"

1. Peel off gift seal from front cover. Place it in space provided at right. This automatically entitles you to receive 2 FREE BOOKS and a fabulous mystery gift.

2. Send back this card and you'll get 2 brand-new Harlequin Temptation® novels. These books have a cover price of $3.99 each in the U.S. and $4.50 each in Canada, but they are yours to keep absolutely free.

3. There's no catch. You're under no obligation to buy anything. We charge nothing—ZERO—for your first shipment. And you don't have to make any minimum number of purchases—not even one!

4. The fact is, thousands of readers enjoy receiving their books by mail from the Harlequin Reader Service®. They enjoy the convenience of home delivery...they like getting the best new novels at discount prices BEFORE they're available in stores...and they love their *Heart to Heart* subscriber newsletter featuring author news, horoscopes, recipes, book reviews and much more!

5. We hope that after receiving your free books you'll want to remain a subscriber. But the choice is yours—to continue or cancel, any time at all! So why not take us up on our invitation, with no risk of any kind. You'll be glad you did!

6. Don't forget to detach your FREE BOOKMARK. And remember...just for validating your Editor's Free Gift Offer, we'll send you THREE gifts, *ABSOLUTELY FREE!*

GET A
FREE MYSTERY GIFT...

SURPRISE MYSTERY GIFT COULD BE YOURS *FREE* AS A SPECIAL "THANK YOU" FROM THE EDITORS OF HARLEQUIN

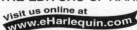

Visit us online at
www.eHarlequin.com

The Editor's "Thank You" Free Gifts Include:

- Two BRAND-NEW romance novels!
- An exciting mystery gift!

PLACE
FREE GIFT
SEAL
HERE

YES! I have placed my Editor's "Thank You" seal in the space provided above. Please send me 2 free books and a fabulous mystery gift. I understand I am under no obligation to purchase any books, as explained on the back and on the opposite page.

342 HDL DNTG   **142 HDL DNS4**

(H-T-06/02)

FIRST NAME	LAST NAME

ADDRESS

APT.#	CITY

STATE/PROV.	ZIP/POSTAL CODE

Thank You!

Offer limited to one per household and not valid to current
Harlequin Temptation® subscribers. All orders subject to approval.

The Harlequin Reader Service® — Here's how it works:

Accepting your 2 free books and gift places you under no obligation to buy anything. You may keep the books and gift and return the shipping statement marked "cancel." If you do not cancel, about a month later we'll send you 4 additional novels and bill you just $3.34 each in the U.S., or $3.80 each in Canada, plus 25¢ shipping & handling per book and applicable taxes if any.* That's the complete price and — compared to cover prices of $3.99 each in the U.S. and $4.50 each in Canada — it's quite a bargain! You may cancel at any time, but if you choose to continue, every month we'll send you 4 more books, which you may either purchase at the discount price or return to us and cancel your subscription.

*Terms and prices subject to change without notice. Sales tax applicable in N.Y. Canadian residents will be charged applicable provincial taxes and GST.

need. In mere seconds, the memory brought her to unbelievable readiness.

She wanted him. Now.

"Show me."

The coffee table creaked again as his laughter sent a ripple of warm breath across her upper thighs. "Oh, I will, sweetheart. I will."

7

JAKE BIT the inside of his cheek hard, sustaining the tight clench of jaw until he tasted blood. God, he wanted to taste her instead. And he would. Soon. Anticipation was working a potent magic on both of them—a magic he hadn't realized he wanted until this moment. A magic he could wield if he retained control.

His heavy breathing didn't help. Each inhalation drew the scent of her arousal into his lungs. Each exhalation caused a ripple of gooseflesh across her bare thighs, a stir of the dark curls around her sweet cleft, like the drawing of a curtain. Inviting yet secretive at the same time.

"Take off the shirt," he ordered.

Her response, a sensual pout, had nothing childish about it. "You said you were going to steal home. You take it off."

He cleared his throat. *Give the woman a little sexual leeway and she gets all sassy.* He loved it, appreciated her attempt to play the game as an equal participant, but he wouldn't surrender the upper hand. Not tonight.

"Uh-uh. I'm the coach. Strip, rookie."

Jake had planned to tell her to remove the shirt slowly, to show her the potent awareness of knowing he was watching her strip at such close range his breath teased her skin. In the stairwell, despite his retelling of his fast and furious fantasy, despite his driving desire to take her, taste her here and now without finesse or delay, he'd claimed he could go slowly. Had he lied? Had he deluded himself about his control? He'd already undressed and slipped on a condom, assuming he couldn't get any harder than he had been since he'd caught her singing before dinner.

He'd been wrong there, too.

Scooting back on the coffee table, Jake forced distance between them, even if only a few inches. He glanced at her face, blindfolded but beautiful. Her skin was flushed, her teeth tugging at her bottom lip in expectation.

Then she smiled. He could tell by the wicked curve of her lips that she intended to comply with his instructions. But given the chance, she might push him further.

She bunched the material from the shoulders, lifting, lifting...revealing, revealing...the natural camber of her belly, the dip of her navel, the gentle swell of her breasts, the hard, dark peaks of her nipples. By the time she tossed the shirt aside, careful not to dislodge the blindfold but throwing her hair into a tumbled mass of sexy disarray, Jake knew precisely where he would kiss her first. Where he *had* to kiss her first.

He braced his hands on her waist, applying one finger at a time so she felt the force of his possession in tantalizing increments.

When he pressed his lips softly against her stomach, she quivered. The flutter quickened his pulse but not his intentions. He placed a kiss over her belly button, then dipped a tad lower for another, then lower for another so his chin skimmed her sensitive curls.

She'd locked her hands behind her neck. If not for the slight movement as she adjusted her stance for better balance, she remained willingly and completely at his command.

Her navel was small, deep and centered with a pearl of flesh he guessed would be sensitive to his tongue. He was right. He mimicked a deep-mouthed kiss until she grasped her hands over his.

"Jake?"

He glanced up. "Hmm?"

"What are you doing?"

"Kissing you."

She licked her lips and huffed her impatience. "No kidding."

"Don't you like it?"

Her hands on his, still poised on her hips, she looked supremely impertinent and annoyed. Oh, and aroused. He couldn't miss that look, even with the blindfold.

"You're a little low. Or high, depending on your perspective."

Jake slipped his hands away from hers, caressing her thighs, stroking her bare bottom, closing his eyes to brand the feel of her in his mind. "Sometimes it's best to start in the middle."

Drawn by her scent, fired by her tiny, pleasured moans, he found the center of her need and in one flash of movement parted her with his tongue. The jolt rocked her balance, but he steadied her with his palms while he explored her with his mouth. Flavors without description danced on his tongue. Her cries of delight resonated over the music, urging him to press her closer, explore further, deeper.

"Oh, Jake. No, I'm going to..."

He knew, and he didn't care. He wanted nothing more than to feel her unravel for him. Completely.

Her hands clutched his shoulders, his back, then speared through his hair, searching for a place to anchor her balance with her equilibrium so unsteady.

Jake knew only one way to steady her. He slid one hand around the back of her thigh and guided one leg onto the table, knee down. He kissed a fiery path to her breasts, loving and laving and sucking her nipples until he had her other leg comfortably tucked beside his thigh, her flesh, moistened by her need and his mouth, poised over the tip of his erection.

He thrust up just as she plunged down. The fire of joining, the electricity of experiencing his sex inside her hot, tight center, jolted him to his feet. In an instant, they were on the couch, her legs locked around his waist while he drove into her with little elegance but explosive results.

She came with his name on her lips, then clutched

his buttocks and urged him deeper, harder, until he did the same. When the sensations spiraled to a quiet, sated lull, he tugged her makeshift blindfold free and watched her eyes adjust to the light.

After licking her lips, she drew in a deep breath and rewarded him with a sly smile. "So...that's stealing home."

"My version." He adjusted their position so he didn't crush her. Just moments ago, he'd forgotten how small she was, how petite. Still, she'd matched his passion thrust for thrust. Across from him, above him or below him, she'd shown him both the depth of her desire and the volume of her strength. He couldn't help but be incredibly impressed.

She cuddled closer, the scent of her hair assailing his nostrils, the smoothness of her bare skin renewing his desire. "I like your version."

"But the question is, did you learn anything useful?"

She ran a finger down a line of hair on his chest, biting her bottom lip. "You're a master with that mouth of yours, though I suspected that earlier in the stairwell."

He bit down an arrogant grin. "What did you learn about eroticism? For your book."

"Quick pacing is a good thing. A *very* good thing," she quipped.

His rumbling laugh felt warm in his belly. He couldn't remember the last time he'd gone from start to finish in such a flash of passion and still enjoyed complete satisfaction beyond the physical release. He wondered how amazing lovemaking would be with Devon if they took things slow...*when* they took things slow.

"What else?"

She drew her hand up to stifle a tiny yawn. "I don't know. I'm too sexually gratified to process the information right now. I usually write down impressions as they occur to me, then sort them out later."

Jake ignored her protests when he eased off the couch, discarded the condom and returned with a pad of paper, a pen and a tiger-print throw blanket he'd pulled from a chair. With open arms, he invited her to snuggle beside him.

"You don't expect me to write, do you?" She took the writing instruments and threw them onto the table, then curled into the crook of his arm. "I'm much too tired, thanks to you."

Jake retrieved them, determined to find out if he'd lived up to her expectations. He knew he'd satisfied her sexually. He wanted to know if he'd met her needs in other areas. Intellectually. For her book.

Aw, hell. He wanted to know if he'd rocked her world the way she had his. He couldn't tell with her acting so damned nonchalant.

"You can dictate. What have you learned so far?"

Her body radiated heat. Her breasts brushed his arm, stirring his desire. He tamped down a groan, determined not to make love to her again tonight, no matter how much either of them wanted to. Not until he could devise a new strategy to top the one they'd just experienced, impossible as it seemed. Besides, if he taught her everything she wanted to know in one night, she might walk away before he was ready. Before he wanted to let her out of his life.

Even now, his mind reeled with disbelief. He couldn't remember ever sitting on a couch with a lover after mind-blowing sex, joking and laughing and teasing. Devon didn't seem the least bit interested in deconstructing what had happened between them or assigning deep emotional meaning that couldn't possibly exist when they'd been lovers for less than a day.

She'd warned him she didn't want a complicated relationship, just an affair, but he hadn't believed her until this very moment. He didn't know why the concept was so hard for him to accept. This wasn't the first time he'd had sex where neither party expected anything more than orgasms. It hadn't bothered him before.

Why did it with Devon?

She retrieved the blindfold from the floor and placed it over her eyes. "I like this blindfold thing. We'll have to do that again."

He jotted the word *blindfold* on the paper. "Why?"

She glared at him until he clarified.

"No, I mean, why do you think the blindfold was so effective? A lot of women would be afraid to try something like that."

"I trusted you not to take advantage. Not in a bad

way," she confessed, tying the blindfold around her head. "I liked the way my other senses heightened to make up for the loss of sight. Oh, and I loved the element of surprise."

"Element of surprise," Jake said as he wrote. "You could use that in a book, right?"

Beneath the bandanna, Devon blinked. *Oh, yeah, the book.* She bit her bottom lip. Exactly what was Jake trying to prove by forcing her to deal with her book when she'd much rather discover a new way to score with him? "I haven't really been thinking about it."

"Shouldn't you? Before you forget?"

Like she was going to forget any detail of this night? Ha!

"I've made copious mental notes, believe me," she said.

"Maybe I should devise a test."

"Maybe you should shut the hell up and kiss me again."

He answered by tearing off the blindfold and lifting her into his arms.

"Not tonight."

"Excuse me? Don't tell me we hit the ninth inning already!"

His chuckle thundered through his chest and into hers. Damn, she loved it when he laughed. She wondered what it would feel like if he laughed while inside her. And she wanted to know. Tonight.

"I'm afraid so, sweetheart. I'm exhausted, and so are you."

She twisted her mouth to keep from yawning again. She hated that he was right, but he was. She hadn't slept much the night before, and the longer she relaxed in his arms, the more the need for sleep ensnared her.

He carried her to his bedroom, kissing her softly along the way, keeping her from arguing with him about what she now knew was an end to the seduction for the night, at least in his mind. He tossed aside the sheets, then laid her gently down.

"What if I don't want to go to sleep? What if I want to make love with you all night long?"

He tilted his eyebrow. "Demanding little minx, aren't you? What's the rush? Why end it all so soon?"

She opened her mouth to speak but didn't have an answer. He was right. He'd told her tonight would be about anticipation, the thrill of stealing home. He'd skillfully shown her that waiting, not knowing, guessing about the next touch, the next kiss, even the next sexual encounter provided the basis for a truly erotic interlude.

Her body still thrummed for him, for his touch, his kiss, his hard shaft buried deep within her. Her mind reeled with the sensations of his mouth exploring her from the inside out, practically worshiping every inch of her. Could she wait for more?

"I won't sleep a wink tonight," she predicted.

Jake grinned. "That makes two of us. But I'll be in the guest room fantasizing about you and you'll be here, snuggled in my bed, conjuring up images of me,

I hope. And we'll only be a few feet and two doorways away."

"What's going to stop me from sneaking into your guest room? Are you going to handcuff me to the bedpost?"

Jake's smile faded, but not the glint in his eyes. "Not tonight. You'll just have to exercise a little self-control."

Devon bristled at his arrogance, but as she watched him swagger out of the room in full naked glory, she guessed his true intentions. A man as proud as he fully understood how to manipulate the same emotion in her. He wanted her to stay put so he threw down the gauntlet of self-control. He wanted to draw out their arrangement. All in all, these were not bad things.

Unless...

Devon was no expert, but Jake's signals, his care and concern, told her he might be acting on something more than lust. Again, not a bad thing. Unless you were Devon Michaels, who wanted a love affair but not the love to go with it.

Not that Devon had anything against the emotion. She wanted to fall in love someday, start a family, build a future that included a soul mate. But the concept, the fantasy, seemed distant, despite her age. She'd long suspected her biological clock had been built digital—no ticking for her. She planned to live life, experience success, enjoy a few dalliances, starting with Jake, before she looked at the possibility of settling down.

She turned off the lamp on the bed stand and snuggled beneath the covers, nude and primed and feeling more sensual than she had in her entire life. She couldn't worry about the long-term complications. High risk or not, she'd definitely done the right thing by taking a chance on Jake Tanner. He was a brilliant teacher. And tomorrow she'd pass whatever test he had for her...and maybe come up with a lesson for him on her own.

"CAN YOU at least tell me what she's looking for? A fling? A lover? A husband?"

Jake cringed. Jillian Hennessy Lawrence, the new wife of his partner, hadn't let up since he'd called their house early this morning and asked for a rare personal favor. Actually, he'd called her husband, Cade, but Cade was out jogging the Bayshore and wasn't due back for at least an hour. Jake had wanted to fetch Devon's car from the Adult High School and return to his apartment as soon as possible. However, once he realized Jillian was his only means to travel, he'd altered his plans. He'd fully expected the grilling he was receiving and had built it into his time frame.

Not that he wanted to tell her one damned thing, but he opted not to fight a fruitless battle. She was the most curious damned woman he'd ever met, next to Devon, of course, particularly in matters that didn't concern her.

"A husband? If she was, she wouldn't be sniffing around me, now would she?"

"What? You can't be a husband? Is there some injury you never told me about?"

Jake coughed and shifted in his seat. Jillian was remarkable and intelligent and attractive, so he could understand how Cade fell so hard, so fast. But she had serious difficulty with the concept of a right to privacy. "Can't? *Won't* is more accurate. Besides, I'm certain she's not in the market for a husband."

Jillian shifted the gear of her midnight-blue Mustang and beat the light at Kennedy and Ashley. "She's single, never married and over thirty. You might want to reassess the clues, detective." Jillian slid her sunglasses down and eyed him carefully even while she watched the light Sunday morning traffic downtown.

"She's not your typical 'over thirty, unmarried so I must be a spinster' woman, Jillian."

"And you know this after one date?"

"It was a long date. And we've actually known each other longer than that."

"A hell of a long date," she reminded him. Jillian and Jake hadn't know each other very long, but she was an intuitive woman who pretty much had him pegged from the first time they'd met. She would know his time in the classroom with Devon had been focused entirely on the course material. He'd only sneaked into Devon's personal space last week, when he'd dared to ask her out and she'd refused but then sent the book with the sexy inscription. "And since she's spent the night at your place, I think it's safe to suspect things are a little more than just casual."

He hadn't meant to let on that Devon had stayed the night, but even if Jillian wasn't a private investigator with finely honed observation skills, she couldn't have missed Devon's purse sitting beside the door or the significance of Jake telling her to knock softly when she arrived at his apartment to pick him up.

"She's spent a good portion of her life raising her sister's kid," he explained. "She hasn't ever been on her own before and she's looking forward to it. So, no, I'm not worried that she wants commitment from me."

She nodded. "I'll buy that. But what do you want?"

"I want to go pick up her car before noon."

"Rather a narrow vision, don't you think?"

"I'm trying not to think, Jillian. That's the point."

Jillian pursed her lips but remained silent for the duration of the drive. Cade had married not only a beautiful woman, but a smart one. She knew when to let a subject drop. Of course, Jake guessed the woman must be a member of Mensa to have figured out how to reel in a man like his partner—who'd once been completely devoted to two things, bachelorhood and undercover work—and to have influenced him to transfer out of the undercover division for more routine detective work.

Not that the TPD faced routine work as a rule, but even after Jake followed Cade out of the undercover squad, Jake knew more than his career had changed. He and Cade had been cut from the same cloth. Both had limited relationships with their families. Both had embraced the military to hone their discipline. Both had joined the force with no other goal than to serve the community, no matter the risk. Or the sacrifice.

Both had eschewed long-term relationships, settling instead for fly-by-night interludes, because turning a woman into a cop's wife was no way to show her you loved her.

Unless she was a woman like Jillian, made of strong Irish stock, capable of protecting herself and focused on her work enough to give Cade the space to do his. She was a special woman. Jake celebrated his buddy's luck at finding someone so uniquely qualified to stand by the side of a man with a badge.

He tried to ignore that Devon wasn't so different from Jillian. She didn't have Jillian's brassy attitude or inherent irreverence, but she did have a similar strength and sense of self. They looked nothing alike, but both knew what they wanted from life and weren't afraid to do what it took to get it.

They had that one up on him. Ever since a stint on the MP squad in the army, he'd wanted to be a cop after his discharge. Since then, he'd served over a decade, had been an exceptional public servant. Now, all that was in jeopardy—because he'd lost the ongoing battle to keep his anger tucked neatly inside. For the first time since his suspension, he allowed himself to consider the possibility of being forced out, even leaving of his own accord.

Jake shook his head, bending forward to turn up the volume of Jillian's radio and block out the direction of his thoughts. Unbidden and insistent, Jake's natural tendency to draw conclusions from both obvious and not-so-obvious clues kept leading him in a direction he didn't want to go.

And not just thoughts of his professional situation.

There was also Devon. He'd promised her their affair would be temporary. No strings. No expectations beyond the sensual. He couldn't go back on his word.

As they drove into the parking lot, empty except for Devon's Escalade, Jillian turned down the music, shifted the car into neutral and pulled up the parking brake.

"There's a bag in the back seat, stuff Cade said you wanted."

Jake reached back and retrieved the brown paper bag, stapled shut and probably filled with files on the unsolved cases his department meant for him to reopen. He'd look at them later. Right now, he just wanted to get the hell out of Jillian's car before she started trying to solve the mysteries of his love life again.

He could damn well solve those himself, thank you very much. Besides, there weren't many unknowns involved. Devon wanted to learn about sex and eroticism, and he wanted to teach her. Simple. Case closed.

Jillian apparently didn't share his viewpoint. "Jake, I've been doing surveillance long enough to read a man's face, even yours when you forget that I'm watching. You really like her, this mysterious mystery writer."

Jake got out and dug into his pocket for Devon's car keys. He considered not answering Jillian. He did have a reputation for being fairly taciturn and guessed she'd laugh off his nonanswer as typical. But Jake didn't know if he was satisfied with his old ways anymore. He had no illusions. His careful control of every action and reaction, his tight rein on his emotions and his insistence on perfection had done little except build walls that were beginning to crumble. He felt penned, trapped. No more a free and happy man than the young boy who'd received biblical board games for his birthday, rather than coveted toys.

"Yes, Jillian, I do really like her. She's the sexiest, most liberating woman I've ever met. The question is, does that matter?"

Jake could see the fact that he'd opened up even that small bit knocked Jillian speechless. Jake chuckled, slammed the car door and jogged to Devon's sport utility vehicle, disengaging the alarm and adjusting the position of the driver's seat before he folded himself inside. He started the engine and rolled down the window.

"Thanks for the ride, Jillian."

She scrambled to lower her window to shout a response, but Jake drove away before she had a chance. He'd posed an important question, he knew that. But he also knew the only person who could answer it was him. And he meant to do so, very, very soon.

8

DEVON WASN'T entirely surprised to wake up to an empty apartment. In fact, she was grateful for the silence. A little space, some daylight quiet time seemed entirely in order after a night of battling what she could best describe as internal combustion.

Long after midnight, she'd struggled with knowing that Jake was only a few footsteps away. She hoped he was thinking about her, reliving their brief but powerful sensual adventure. The warmth of his kisses heated her body in defiance of the low air-conditioner setting. The slick trails from his tongue bathed her in a hot, lusty rush. She snuggled in sheets peppered with his spicy scent and wished they'd made love a second time more slowly, so she could savor the sensations instead of relying on her memories, powerful though they were.

She'd drifted to sleep, but the erotic content of her dreams invariably stirred her awake. Sometimes she woke softly, like when she dreamed of returning his ministrations, kissing the entire length and full width of his body until her mouth went dry with need. Sometimes she practically leaped out of bed with a jolt, particularly from the dream where they made love in a dugout during a World Series matchup, his hard length crashing into her to the sound of a bat cracking and the crowd roaring.

She hadn't had the energy to jot down her impressions or sneak into the living room to retrieve Jake's scribbles. Instead, she'd remained in bed, content in the darkness to relive every detail, vowing to make sure she experienced each and every one again.

Shortly after seven o'clock, Jake had left his bedroom. Twenty minutes later, he left the apartment. Raising a teenager had honed Devon's sense of hearing to hypersensitive perfection. Unfortunately, raising that same teenager had also caused her to ignore her own needs for so long, she'd developed an acute case of lust for a man who was obviously determined to drive her insane simply by adhering to the deal they'd made. Erotic experiences, one at a time, with no strings attached.

She'd slept as Jake had left her the night before, naked, part of her sated and exhausted, part of her primed for more. Her nipples chafed against the soft cotton sheets, but she decided she could live with the discomfort for a while longer. It was, after all, a new day. With a wry and wicked grin, she rolled out of his bed and headed to Jake's bathroom for a hot shower, then dug into his T-shirts for clean cover. With no idea how long Jake would be gone, she figured she'd be in better condition if she didn't wallow in his musky scent.

She gathered her jeans, blouse and lingerie from the

day before, rolled them into a ball and sought his washing machine. Padding around his apartment in nothing more than his shirt was okay for the moment, but sooner or later she'd have to get herself home.

She did, after all, have work to do.

After heading to the kitchen to seek out a laundry closet of some sort, she wondered if Jake intended her to leave before their next erotic encounter. On the breakfast bar, beside a freshly brewed pot of coffee and the notes he'd taken the night before, gleamed the LCD screen of a fairly new model laptop computer. The screen saver twirled in rainbow colors. A message said, "Read Me, Devon."

She clicked the touch pad and found a note from Jake, typed in all caps and with no punctuation but subtle nonetheless.

TIME TO PUT YOUR NEW KNOWLEDGE TO GOOD USE

She raised an eyebrow and dropped the laundry on the breakfast bar. In all her adult years, she'd never met one single man who truly understood writers or artists unless he was a writer or artist himself. The need to apply new ideas to a chosen medium before inspiration disappeared into the creative ether forced her to keep a notepad inside every purse she owned and a tape recorder in her car. Her laptop stayed on beside her bed, just in case the solution to her latest plot dilemma emerged during the night.

Yet she'd resisted working with all the new ideas Jake had inspired, as if committing them to paper would somehow betray the intimacy she and Jake had begun to develop. She knew her book had been the impetus for their affair, and success still meant the world to her, but tearing down the wall of one compartment of her life—her work—and merging the contents with her new sexual discoveries still seemed wrong somehow. Jake, however, obviously didn't have a problem with her applying her new knowledge immediately. He'd fairly ordered her to get to work, in his own charming way.

Well, she had promised to oblige the man.

She found the washing machine in a closet beside the guest bathroom and loaded her jeans and panties in for a quick wash, along with a few T-shirts and shorts she found in Jake's hamper. After pouring a mug of coffee and snagging a bagel from his freezer to heat in the toaster oven, she scooped up the laptop and set up shop on his dining room table. Not surprisingly, he'd cleared away the mess from the night before, leaving nothing to distract her.

By the time she heard his key in the door, she'd written ten pages. Ten damned good pages—the beginning of a sexual interlude between Leah, her heroine, and Leah's sexy cop lover. In a stairwell. During a rainstorm.

"You take direction very well, don't you?" he said, locking the door behind him and hooking his keys on the rack beside the stereo.

Devon clicked the save icon, then lowered the screen. She intended to show Jake her work, maybe even garner his approval, but not just yet. She hoped to stir his curiosity. Draw things out. Last night, she'd thought she'd be satisfied with exploring her attraction to Jake in one fell swoop, but after sampling the power of his influence on her creative juices, she abandoned her previous preference for speed. In all her years of focusing on the here and now, on enjoying the benefits of instant gratification, courtesy of her sister's wealth, she had forgotten the value of anticipation. She wondered what Jake had planned next and how much time he had to give her.

"Doesn't take much to inspire me to work, Jake."

His scowl made her smile. She wasn't lying. She loved to work. She particularly loved to work when the words flowed from her like water from a faucet. Didn't happen often, but when it did, she always felt like celebrating with a silly dance, chocolate and a bottle of Asti Spumante. Funny, but that didn't seem as appealing today, not when she and Jake could cook up something much more intoxicating.

"Should I be insulted?" he asked.

"Not in the least! How hard is it for you to roll out of bed in the morning to drive to the precinct after spending most of the night on a stakeout?"

Jake nodded but didn't say a word. Instead, he marched by, clutching a large paper grocery bag. A chilly awareness swept over her skin. His body language mirrored the answer she'd expected—that he loved his work and, even when exhausted, looked forward to hitting his beat. But something in his eyes, something so subtle anyone less than a trained people watcher might have missed it, caused her to wonder.

Damn. Had she really been so blind? So wrapped up in her needs and problems that she'd failed to spot something amiss with the devoted but suspended detective?

The day before, he'd told her about the incident with the wife beater, but his actions had seemed so justified to her she'd barely given the episode a second thought. She knew suspension was routine in such cases and that after an internal investigation Jake might receive a letter of reprimand to his file, but he'd be back on the force in no time. She wondered if that's what he wanted.

She'd promised both Sydney and herself that, at least for this time with Jake, she'd push away her natural tendency to put other people's needs above her own. She'd done that her entire life and ended up starved for a little success, a little pleasure to call hers and hers alone. She didn't regret caring for her mother or for Cassie, but she did regret not taking care of herself at the same time. Devon only knew how to do one thing at a time—a definite disadvantage in a world prone to multitasking.

So here was her chance to learn how to balance. Yes, she wanted to learn more about her sexuality and couldn't wait to find out what Jake planned next. But at the same time, she intended to find out precisely what haunted Jake Tanner, what lived in the shadows she'd seen behind his eyes.

And maybe, just maybe, she'd find a way to help him let in the light.

JAKE MARCHED into his bedroom, forgetting he'd turned it over to Devon until he realized his dirty clothes were no longer spilling out of the hamper in the corner and the scent of his shampoo, mixed with her natural perfume, lingered in the air. On the bed, he set down the bag Jillian had given him, a bag he knew most certainly did not contain department case files. Instead, he'd discovered an array of sensual oils, lotions and toys, all lemon-scented and flavored.

He'd known Jillian tended to bend the truth when it suited her, but he never figured her for a matchmaker. Seemed way too blatantly female for a woman who held a black belt and possessed the know-how to hack into the most guarded personal information stored in any computer, anywhere, if she needed to.

Women like Jillian Hennessy Lawrence shouldn't spend their time snooping into his love life.

The scent of lemons from the paper bag had piqued his curiosity while he'd driven around aimlessly, trying to come up with an inventive way to lure Devon to their next erotic encounter. When he'd peeked in the bag, he'd sent Jillian a mental thank-you. The woman was obviously clever in more ways than one. He hoped his partner knew how lucky he was.

"What's in the bag?"

Devon leaned on the doorjamb, his army T-shirt hanging nearly to her knees, her hair wavy and still a little damp on the ends, her face scrubbed free of all makeup. She'd been stunning the day before with her tight, sexy clothes, dark eyeliner and hot pink lips. Today, she exuded a beauty that reminded him of one of the early days in a Florida autumn, his favorite time of year. Crisp and clear. Blue skies and green leaves and a nip in the air that invigorated rather than chilled.

"A present from a friend of mine."

"Is it your birthday?"

Jake shook his head, curling the top of the bag closed as tightly as he could. "No birthday. Jillian is just a very generous woman. The gift is actually for both of us."

Generous and interfering. He never would have guessed. Since they'd met, Cade and Jillian seemed utterly and totally wrapped up in themselves and their new romance. Jake marveled that they'd managed to track down a criminal at the same time they'd forged the relationship that led to their marriage. An enthusiastic newlywed, Jillian had still made time to encourage Jake's romance. Only it wasn't a romance, was it? Just an affair.

"Jillian?" Devon asked.

Either Devon didn't try to disguise the jealousy in her voice or she had no idea how annoyed she sounded by speaking the three syllables.

Jake puffed at the surge to his ego.

Devon crossed her arms over her chest. "My erotic education isn't going to include a second person, is it?"

Jake nearly choked at the thought, adding a laugh to his cough to cover his shock. Like any living, breathing man, Jake had sometimes entertained three-some fantasies, but never with Devon. He didn't intend to share her with anyone.

"Jillian isn't that kind of friend, Devon. But if that's what you're into..."

Devon rolled her eyes at his suggestion and waved the innuendo away with her hand. "Yeah, the woman who hadn't been kissed by a man in a good five years now wants to share her lover with another woman. Logic, Jake." She tapped her temple. "Don't forget the logic."

He laughed, then took the bag and shoved it in his closet. While the idea of Devon turning territorial stoked his self-confidence, the reality of her wanting to keep him entirely to herself fired him even more.

"Jillian is my partner's wife. I called Cade to drive me down to the school to get your car, but he wasn't home. She filled in."

"And she knew enough to bring us a gift?"

"Jillian always seems to know more than she should. I've learned not to question her means, and since I think her gift is fairly brilliant, I'm not questioning her intentions, either. Because I asked her to help, she knew you stayed with me last night. And because my partner has taken his marriage vows about being open and honest way too seriously, she also knows that I've had my eye on you for weeks."

There. He watched his admission inject itself

straight into her, watched her smile bloom a little brighter. He'd also effectively distracted her from asking more about the bag and Jillian's gift—at least temporarily.

"I never heard anything in the marriage vows about being open and honest," Devon said, her expression perplexed.

Jake slid the closet door closed and joined Devon in the doorway. "They wrote their own vows. If you knew the details of their courtship, the wording wouldn't surprise you."

She turned, leaning on her hands. He mirrored her stance, spreading his feet so he didn't tower over her so much.

"Someday you'll have to fill me in."

"But not today?"

She licked her lips. "Aren't you curious about what I wrote this morning?"

Wildly curious, but he didn't think she'd be so quick to offer a peek. When his sister wrote anything, she guarded her words with her life until she'd reworked and reworded to her impossibly high standards. Even when she'd left journalism and given him her practically new laptop, which he hadn't used until he'd set it up for Devon this morning, Kat deleted each and every file that contained any of her articles.

Apparently, either Devon possessed a great deal more assurance in her work, or she trusted Jake not to judge her.

He guessed the answer was both.

"I can't wait."

The sound of a mechanical ding broke the silence, and Jake suddenly realized that the compact dryer tucked into the hall closet had been adding to the heat he'd been experiencing since joining Devon in the hallway.

"First, the laundry," she said, rolling away. "Wouldn't want your clothes to get all wrinkled, now, would you?"

Jake watched with utter fascination as Devon sauntered down the hall and proceeded to remove one of his shirts from the dryer, taking a long sniff before she snapped the material smooth and folded it with quick precision. With a bit of a shock, he realized he'd assumed a woman who lived in a house like hers had servants to do such mundane things as wash and fold laundry. Perhaps she did. But he doubted that Devon, a woman raised in near poverty, flourishing in her sister's wealth and determined to build her own security, minded a few chores.

Still, chores were more fun when done with someone else.

He sidled up, his interest piqued when she handed him her jeans to fold.

"I hope these haven't shrunk in the wash," he quipped. "I don't think you'll be able to squeeze into them."

She continued folding without missing a beat. "I assume you're not saying I've gained weight since yesterday."

Jake grabbed a T-shirt from the pile. "You assume correctly."

"Didn't you like my dressed-for-seduction choices?"

"I did. May I make a suggestion for our next... session?"

She stopped folding long enough to study his face, gauge his intentions. Jake didn't bother hiding the wicked gleam in his eyes. Jillian's mystery gift spurred Jake's imagination in ways he hadn't thought possible. Men, by his estimation, weren't particularly imaginative when it came to sex. Even the fantasy he'd told Devon about in the stairwell was a cliché, particularly when the man behind the fantasy was a cop.

Well, things were about to change. Devon Michaels made her living with her imagination. The least he could do was push his boundaries a bit.

"By all means, suggest away. However, you have to remember that my wardrobe is limited right now to one pair of jeans—a size too small—one pair of panties, a blouse that is still in need of a good washing and a missing bra."

Jake remembered the missing bra. He'd tucked the pilfered undergarment into his sock drawer, the primary location for all things collectible.

"I can't believe I'm going to say this." He finished folding the last shirt, then exhaled with a huge, overly frustrated breath.

"What?"

He grasped her by her shoulders. "This may be a real hardship for you...but let's go shopping."

DEVON REALIZED that Jake had made more than one assumption about her nature as a woman based on the knowledge he'd gleaned from the one constant woman in his life—his sister. While Devon acknowledged that she and Kat Tanner probably had enough in common to get along reasonably well, they also possessed great differences. For one, Devon hated shopping. Loathed it. She had assumed her aversion started a long time ago when she never had enough money to buy anything, but even after Darcy set her up in the house and gave her a credit card with an open limit, Devon still hadn't understood the allure. Buying, she discovered, hadn't been her problem. The search, the hunt for the perfect item—that she had no patience for.

Jake, however, had already taught her a thing or two about patience. And she certainly wasn't going to admit any negative feelings about going to the mall—not when Jake had such an intriguing look swimming in those intoxicating whiskey eyes.

The man was up to something...and she couldn't wait to see exactly what he had in mind.

"I'll have to squeeze into my jeans," she pointed out.

He stroked his chin, clean shaven but square enough to look rugged even when smooth and bare. "I am at your service if you need help."

I'll just bet you are. "I should borrow a clean shirt from you...and maybe coax you into returning my bra?"

He leaned a hip on the washer and crossed his arms over his thick chest. "Pick any shirt you like, but consider the bra gone for good."

She matched his stance, just as he'd done in the doorway. Establishing equal footing seemed a pattern with them, one Devon found particularly fascinating.

"And I'm hungry," she said. "I can't shop on an empty stomach."

Jake's grin spread across his face, and Devon decided that when the man allowed himself to experience a full breadth of amusement, he was handsome enough to make most women weep.

"Works for me. The mall doesn't open until noon."

Devon couldn't remember the last time she'd been coaxed into a mall, the bastion of shopaholic Nirvana. Over a year ago, at least, when Tampa's first truly upscale gathering of boutiques and department stores opened near the airport and she'd done a book signing, then spent a few hours browsing windows with Cassie. She bit her bottom lip, certain that gazing into stylized window displays with Jake would be so much more interesting.

"I'll get dressed then," she said, snagging her jeans and panties from atop the dryer. "This better be good, Tanner. You have no idea how the idea of walking around in a crowded mall doesn't appeal to me."

She heard Jake chuckle behind her, the sound luring her to turn and watch his eyes darken to the color of unmistakable wickedness. "Don't worry, Devon. I intend to make the sacrifice worth your while."

9

SO THIS WAS Frederick's of Hollywood. Jake hadn't anticipated such a classy overall look. His expectations stemmed from his experience busting illegal massage parlors that doubled as lingerie stores and the sexy, somewhat raunchy catalogues that had permanent residence in the men's room at the precinct. Not quite as lacy and feminine as Victoria's Secret, Frederick's of Hollywood in the University Square Mall sold seduction and good-natured naughtiness amid gleaming mirrors, shiny chrome displays and a rainbow of silky selections that made no apologies for being both titillating and outrageous.

"Okay, we're here," Devon said, hooking her thumbs in her front pockets. "Start suggesting."

She gazed at him with total innocence and blatant high hopes. Jake didn't pretend to know what he wanted, so he grinned warmly at the attractive saleswoman who immediately approached and hoped she'd nudge them in the right direction—with a minimum of embarrassment, of course.

"Can I help you?"

Jake mirrored Devon's casual stance, determined to appear as if shopping for sexy lingerie was something he did every day. "Yes, you can. I'm looking to buy some pretty things for this beautiful lady."

The woman sighed audibly. "Most men are too embarrassed to come in here."

Jake cleared his throat. "Most men are fools."

"Can't argue that," the saleswoman said with a smirk. "Come on, sweetheart." She turned to Devon. "What kind of lingerie do you think this big handsome hunk of yours would like?"

Devon handed him her purse and winked. "Let's start with bras."

Jake had taken the reins to this moment, suggesting the shopping excursion, choosing the store and greeting the salesclerk. He found a soft leather chair near the dressing rooms, content to allow Devon to stretch her imagination and construct a sensual surprise. He watched her paw through racks of colorful, sheer and lacy contraptions. After bras, she looked at nighties, gowns and teddies, selecting several for the saleswoman to take to the dressing room.

Once she was inside, he closed his eyes, imagining her undressing, then swathing herself in peekaboo silk and satin. He'd once arrested a couple for making love in a dressing room at a local department store. And while he understood the allure—all those mirrors and the thrill of possible discovery—he'd never shared that particular fantasy. Until now.

When Devon's purse trilled, he glanced at the door. On the second ring, Devon popped her head out.

He caught a flash of bright green. "Is that my phone?"

Jake held up her purse. "Sounds like it."

"Can you grab it? It might be Cassie. It's in the zippered part."

Jake pulled out the phone and handed it to her. Through the opening of the door, he spied something silky in an electric royal blue, the same color as her eyes.

His mouth went dry.

"Thanks."

Her hand lingered on his, her fingers brushing his wrist, making the hair on his entire arm stir from the gooseflesh. She glanced inside the dressing room, then shut the door. After a moment, he heard her curse. The phone kept ringing. She hadn't answered it.

He leaned close so he didn't have to shout. "Is something wrong?"

"No," she said, her tone exasperated. "It's not Cassie. It's Sydney."

"Sydney the romance writer?" Jake remembered them discussing her friend sometime over the past few hours, but he couldn't remember any details other than her occupation and the fact that she'd encouraged Devon to go after Jake. He had to remember to thank the woman profusely if they ever met.

The phone trilled one last time.

"Why didn't you answer it?"

"She'll call back."

"That's not what I asked."

The door to the dressing room was tall, with tight slats that allowed him to see no more of Devon than a few flashes of color.

"She'll want details. She'll want to know if I came home last night. She'll want to know if we made love and what I'm doing right now."

Jake marveled that Devon seemed so reluctant to share. Wasn't she, after all, chronicling the nuances of their affair to enhance the eroticism of her book, a novel that could ultimately reach millions of readers? He'd already figured out that so long as she changed the names, he wouldn't mind having their love life immortalized in a book. No one would really know but the two of them.

And, apparently, this Sydney woman.

The phone began chirping again.

"She's nothing if not persistent," Devon said with an exasperated sigh.

"Do you want to talk to her?"

"Not right this minute, no."

Jake pushed aside the feeling that he'd reverted to high school and easily reached over the top of the door. "Then give me the phone."

DEVON COULDN'T HELP smiling all the way to the car. With her purchases—Jake's purchases, since he'd insisted on paying the bill for the lingerie he'd yet to see—wrapped in soft tissue paper and tucked into several glossy shopping bags, she felt like a true adventurer, alive and invigorated and in possession of priceless secret bounty.

And not just because of the new bras, panties and teddies, or the clothes and sandals Jake had insisted she buy when they walked through Dillards department store. He suggested she stock up so she didn't have to go home anytime soon. Not that she had any desire to head back to her old life. As much as she loved that big mansion and the privacy and safety it symbolized, the freedom and casual comfort of Jake's apartment suited her just fine. For the moment. And only as long as Jake wanted her in his life.

Apparently, Jake had handled Sydney like a pro. He'd returned her phone, and it hadn't rung since. Devon loved her friend with all her heart, but she didn't have the energy to focus on eluding Sydney's interminable quest for details.

Unfortunately, Devon hadn't been able to hear what must have been a fascinating conversation. Jake traded her purse for the phone and disappeared into the common area of the mall. He returned twenty minutes later, just in time to hand the saleswoman his credit card.

"Sydney wants you to call her when you get home," was all he'd said.

She resisted asking about what they'd discussed but warmed at his take-charge attitude nonetheless. Devon had never in her life been rescued. Yes, her sister's success and wealth had saved them from living on welfare for the rest of their lives, or worse, committing Cassie to foster care, but the lifeline was more for the family than for Devon personally.

She was making too much of his actions, she knew. Jake had averted an uncomfortable phone conversation. In fact, she should be feeling like a coward for avoiding her best friend who would have understood, albeit with a heavy dose of bitching, if Devon said she couldn't talk to her. Instead, Devon remained grateful to Jake. Talking to Sydney would have been too real in the midst of her fantasy shopping spree. At the moment, she didn't want to be reminded of her initial reluctance to pursue Jake or admit, however true it was, that she did indeed have a lot to learn from him.

But still, no matter how she tried not to subscribe to an overly romantic image of Jake, she couldn't help looking at him like a valiant knight in shining armor. Sydney could be a damned intimidating force, particularly with men. She usually got what she wanted when she wanted it—and sometimes before she even asked. However, Jake had apparently handled her with ease.

"What are you grinning about?" he asked as they opened the doors between the department store and the covered parking garage. A blast of hot, humid air greeted them. The weather was clear, the sky practically cloudless. But the moisture from yesterday's rain seemed to linger, inspiring Devon's pores to sweat the moment they ventured outside.

"Did I thank you for talking to Sydney?" she asked, knowing she hadn't and knowing she should have.

"I wouldn't be so quick to show gratitude," Jake said cryptically. "You have no idea what I told her."

Mischief danced in his eyes, but Devon wasn't fooled. Jake protected his privacy almost as much as she did hers. He wouldn't have told Sydney anything intimate—at least, not anything true. Devon wouldn't have put it past him to invent a story or two just to keep Sydney at bay.

"I hope you told her I might not be calling for a while."

He pointed toward the row where he'd parked her Escalade. "That I did. She didn't seem the least bit worried, either."

"She knows I can take care of myself. But she's probably suffering from a raging case of curiosity right now. It might kill her."

"She'll survive."

Devon watched his face, wondering if he had concocted some scenarios to entertain Sydney's insatiable nosiness, but he didn't reveal anything. She shrugged, figuring Sydney could benefit from having Jake yank her chain. As much as she loved her best friend and appreciated her expertise in the male-female interaction area, the woman manipulated men with way too much ease and was in serious need of a lesson in plain, old-fashioned humility.

Talk about humility, she thought the minute she caught sight, yet again, of her beautiful sport utility vehicle, which she'd purchased with the royalties from her last book. The black paint, tainted by a thick film of caked road dust and rain splatters, had lost the glossy sleekness that had attracted her in the first place.

"You can't stand to see this car dirty, can you?"

She laughed at her compulsive attitude but didn't deny it, knowing she'd grimaced as she approached. "I love this car. I had Darcy install one of those self-service type car washes at the house so I could keep it all neat and tidy."

"You don't have someone to wash your car for you?"

Devon snorted. "That's all I need, a bunch of strangers to look after. Darcy is the one with the entourage. Cassie and I usually manage to take care of ourselves. I do have a woman who comes in twice a week, only because the house is too damned big for me to keep dusted and vacuumed. But no nannies, no cooks, no butler, unless Darcy is in for a visit."

"No nanny? How did you go to school with a baby to take care of?"

Jake pulled the keys out of his pocket, disengaged the security alarm and opened Devon's door. She hopped in, filing the packages into the space near her feet.

"We had someone back then, but once I finished school, I preferred to do things on my own. What about you?"

"I had a housekeeper once, but I guess the cop in me didn't like someone poking around in my stuff. So

I do things myself. It's the price of being a bachelor, I guess."

"You do fairly well, for a guy. Your mother must have taught you well."

"She did the best she could with me, that's for sure."

Jake slammed her door shut and jogged to the driver's side. Devon thought Mrs. Tanner had done a darned remarkable job. Jake was a rare combination of man—a gentleman and trustworthy public servant on one hand and a risk-taking adventurer on the other. Somewhere underneath those two warring images, Devon figured, the real Jake Tanner existed.

"You know, you haven't mentioned your mother until now."

He placed the key in the ignition and snapped on his seat belt before he responded. "My mother is salt of the earth. A little submissive to my dad, but she's happy that way."

"Do you talk to her often?"

Jake's mouth pursed, and Devon knew she had to push. While she hadn't seen another indication of those shadows she'd glimpsed, she guessed that delving into Jake's past, into his relationships with his family and friends, was key to understanding the man he'd become, the man who'd been suspended for breaking a hard-and-fast rule of never losing his cool. Jake had agreed to teach her about eroticism, but he didn't seem so open to exploring anything about himself beyond the surface. She had a desire to know what he wanted from life. What he needed.

As much as she still hoped to keep her relationship with Jake temporary, she couldn't deny the man had gotten under her skin. She cared about him, and probably had for quite some time. Learning Jake's secrets jumped up on the list of Devon's priorities. He seemed determined to satisfy her needs, both sexual and professional. But he had hardly given her a clue about what she could offer him in return.

"Jake?"

His name was enough of a prod. With one of his sweet half grins, he turned the engine over and admitted, "I speak to her about once a week. We don't talk about anything earth-shattering but exchange the usual pleasantries—how are you, I'm fine, how's the weather. Makes her happy just knowing I haven't been killed in the line of duty and no one told her."

"She sounds like a sweet woman."

"She's your typical God-fearing preacher's wife with a heart as big as the farmland she was born on."

"And your father?"

Jake turned his attention to navigating out of the parking lot. "I've told you about him."

Not much. "A hard man to please?"

Jake inhaled deeply and nodded, acknowledging that she'd hit the nail on the head.

"At least you have a father."

He raised his eyebrows.

"Well, I had a father, I just never knew him. He

never married our mother and left right after learning Mom was pregnant with me."

"Does that bother you?"

"Used to. But if he'd ever wanted to find us again, he could have. Especially after Darcy made it big. We've never heard a word, which is just as well."

"How do you know he's still alive?"

Devon shrugged, loath to admit she'd tracked her father down through the Internet several years ago. From what she'd learned, he had a somewhat steady job as a blackjack dealer in a casino, had never married and had a decent credit rating. She'd been surprised to realize that the smidgen of information had been enough to satisfy her curiosity.

"He's alive. I've never experienced a need to know him. His actions spoke loud and clear. He didn't want a family. So, I moved along...although having a wayward father does makes a girl a little leery of dating, when you figure you might end up inadvertently sleeping with a half brother or something."

Jake let loose a shocked laugh. "Who thinks of those things?"

"My sister. Me. Did you know Darcy hired Cassie's father as a roadie as soon as she made it big, just to keep an eye on him?"

Jake shook his head. "Your sister sounds a little controlling."

She shrugged. "Yeah, well, she's had to be. He doesn't know about Cassie. And the lughead obviously is too dense to do simple math, though Cassie really doesn't look anything like him."

"Does Cassie know who he is?"

"Oh, yeah. Darcy told her about him when she was six or seven, but it's weird—she's never shown any interest in knowing him. Darcy told Cassie she could decide when to let him in on her paternity, and she's never wanted to. She told me once that her mother and I did pretty damned good without a father in our lives, so she figured she could do the same. I don't know if that's healthy, but it's her choice. She's eighteen now, and the choice hasn't changed."

"Can't blame her. If it ain't broke, don't fix it, right?"

Jake glanced at her, then drove past the Steak n Shake where they'd had a late breakfast before going to the mall. They'd chatted easily during the meal, Devon aware she had done most of the talking, all on topics that could be discussed in public—explaining how book royalties and advances worked, sharing humorous anecdotes about bookstore appearances, telling more stories about raising her niece than a die-hard single male probably ever wanted to hear. But he'd been an ardent and active listener, amusing her with a few tales of his adventures with Cade on various stings and stakeouts. He'd told her about how Cade and Jillian had met during a case of hidden identities. Otherwise, Jake seemed content to let her provide the bulk of personal revelations.

Well, enough was enough.

"But how do you fix things that *are* broken?" she asked.

He glanced sideways, his gaze on the road but his attention on her. "That's a loaded question, isn't it?" he asked.

"Caught red-handed."

He slowed for a stoplight. "What's broken that needs fixing? I haven't disappointed you already, have I?"

Devon rolled her eyes but experienced a rush of pleasure that even the serious turn of their conversation hadn't taken his mind off their next sexual encounter, specifically for which she'd purchased some silk and lace. "Disappointed? Hardly. I'm incredibly impressed with your techniques. Can't wait to see what you've got in mind next."

"No more than I can wait to see what you bought. The suspense is killing me."

She wiggled her eyebrows. "I assure you, detective, the torture will be worth your while. But I was alluding to your suspension. You haven't said anything about it since yesterday."

"What more is there to say? Internal Affairs should make a decision about my fate sometime this week."

"What do you think they'll say?"

Jake maneuvered around a late-model Plymouth.

"I haven't thought about it much."

She clucked her tongue. "You don't actually expect me to believe that, do you?"

"It's the truth. I'm not saying the incident hasn't

been food for thought. But the department's reaction, my punishment...I haven't lost too much sleep over it. Whatever happens, happens. I'm prepared to accept the consequences."

"Even if it means being kicked off the force?"

Jake felt his breath hitch, but he was careful to hide the reaction from Devon, which wasn't so difficult since he'd been hiding the impending sense of dread from himself for over a week. He wasn't lying. He hadn't allowed himself to dwell on the possibility of leaving the force. How could he? All he'd ever wanted to be was a soldier and a cop. He'd defied family tradition to pursue his dream. He'd loved every hot, sweaty minute of his stint in the army and for the bulk of his career had cherished the chance to serve as a cop. But lately, even before his suspension, he'd wondered how much longer he wanted to collar criminals who hired high-priced attorneys to beat the system and return to their thieving ways. He'd spent months of twenty-five-hour days building ironclad cases that fell apart in the hands of inexperienced prosecutors. He'd been haunted by more than one battered face, by the indelible frown of a child who'd seen more ugliness in less than a decade than most people saw in a half century.

It was a lot to face, a lot of think about, and Jake hadn't wanted to put in the effort. Devon, on the other hand, wore her emotions and her intentions plainly. She knew what she wanted from life, just like he used to. She knew what she wanted from her career, just like he used to. He admired the traits in her, but he wasn't certain he could match her candor. He wasn't certain he had the guts to quit and try something new.

"I can appeal," he answered.

"So you don't want to leave police work?"

Jake cleared his throat. She'd asked the question with such a confident sound, as if she'd somehow crept into his psyche and witnessed the constant flashing of that question in his mind. He'd already learned that she was an intuitive woman, that she watched the people around her with open eyes, but he hadn't expected her to clue in to a dilemma he hadn't fully faced.

He decided to answer truthfully. From the start, they'd established a pattern of honest disclosure. Jake, a self-acclaimed creature of habit, decided to stick to what worked. "I don't know."

She nodded, obviously content to let the topic drift, as if she knew what the admission had cost him. If he'd been a romantic man, he would have interpreted the leap in his chest as the contents of his heart shifting, squeezing out another trace of the darkness pumping there to make more room for her. But as a pragmatist, he decided the sensation was an increase in his already burgeoning desire.

At the interstate, Jake steered the car into the northbound lane. The idea for an afternoon adventure sprung into his mind so quickly, he didn't have the time to question.

"Where are we going?" Devon asked.

Jake winked. "How do you feel about the out-doors?"

"Trees and flowers are very nice," she answered, her tone wary.

"Does this car have four-wheel drive?"

"Yes." She narrowed her gaze. "Why?"

"Ever tried it out?"

"The four-wheel drive? Of course not. I wanted a black Escalade, and the only black one on the lot had four-wheel drive."

Jake chuckled. Every ounce an unapologetic woman, his Devon.

His Devon. Lord, how that term summed up more than he was willing to admit.

"What do you say we try it out?"

"Does this have anything to do with my lingerie or the scent of lemons coming from that mysterious gift from Jillian that you chucked in the back seat when you thought I wasn't looking?"

Observant and curious. A potent combination, par-ticularly when mixed with the ingredients of Freder-ick's of Hollywood and lemon-scented massage lo-tion. Jake couldn't wait to show her how inventive and imaginative this cop could be.

"All of the above, Ms. Michaels."

"Really? Well then, by all means, let's explore the great outdoors."

10

DEVON WASN'T CERTAIN she'd ever walk again, but so long as she had Jake around to carry her, she didn't care. Her backside ached from bouncing around, even on plush, top-of-the-line leather seats. Her knuckles were cramped from clutching the armrest and the handle between the passenger door and the front windshield. She'd always wondered what that handle was for. Now, after going off-roading with Jake in her very expensive, very muddy Cadillac, she knew.

She also knew no man knew how to prime a woman with adrenaline like Jake Tanner. Only he would consider bouncing around the wild Florida landscape, jumping hills and crashing through swampland foreplay. Only a man like Jake could transform such activity into foreplay, and he most certainly had.

Her heart pumped with excitement. Her shoulders ached for the healing massage of his skilled touch. Carrying her through a clump of wild palmettos, he stomped into the brush like some backwoods bridegroom on the way to his honeymoon hideaway. And like a virginal wife unaccustomed to a man's touch, she squealed when one of the fronds swung and slapped her in the ass, causing Jake to laugh for what seemed like the hundredth time in the last hour.

She'd never experienced a more potent aphrodisiac than the rumble of this man's mirth. By the time he set her on the weathered porch of a cabin she would generously describe as rustic, her entire body thrummed with wanting him.

"We're here," he announced.

"I can see that. Where is here, exactly?"

Jake pulled out his key ring, flipping through until he found the key that would open the thick padlock on the door.

"Someplace I haven't been in a long, long time."

Jake hadn't exaggerated. From the look of the motes swirling in the air the minute he pushed open the creaking door, *no one* had been in the cabin for a while. Yet, surprisingly, there wasn't much dust on the floors or the mantel over the stone fireplace. The rugs looked freshly beaten. The cabin, which consisted of one fairly large room with a kitchen area in one corner, a living area with a couch and easy chairs in another and a bedroom with bunks and a dressing screen along the entire side wall, was simple in design. And thanks to a tin roof only partially covered by the trees, stifling hot.

"I'll open the shutters and windows. Why don't you check out the rations?"

"You own this cabin?"

"My mother deeded it to me about ten years ago, after my father bought another fishing cabin closer to home on the other coast. We used to drive down here when I was a kid."

Devon watched Jake efficiently open the windows, unlocking the wood shutters from the inside and swinging them out to let in the fresh air and light. She tried to imagine him as a child, scampering with enthusiasm for a weekend of adventure in the woods. He'd been reticent about sharing the details of his childhood, yet here he was, showing her firsthand an obviously important part of his youth.

"It's fairly clean," she commented, struggling for something to say that wouldn't push him into the caginess that normally overtook him when he talked about his past.

"Mother makes at least a biannual pilgrimage here to clean it out in case I want to use it." He paused, then clicked on the one overhead light attached to a creaky but working ceiling fan. "Personally, I think she enjoys the time away. Sometimes she stays for a couple of days while my father is on retreat or at some conference."

As Jake let more light into the main room, Devon noticed shelf upon shelf of paperbacks. Topics ranged from fantasy and science fiction to classic literature and a nearly complete original set of medical romances by Betty Neels. Devon smiled when she spotted two of her Fioranna DiMarco mysteries among the eclectic collection.

"Do these belong to your mother?"

Jake squinted, then his eyes widened with surprise.

"Yeah, I guess. She's the only person who ever comes here. She always brings a few books. There weren't this many last time I was here."

Either Jake's mother came more than twice a year or the woman was a speed reader. "Your mom comes out here to clean or to read?"

He slung his hands into the pockets of his jeans. "I guess both. Dad's pretty particular about the reading material he allows in the house. I knew Mom didn't always agree with him, but I had no idea...."

Devon filled in the blanks by watching his expression change from shock to amazed disbelief to pride. Apparently, Jake had had no idea his mother had such defiance in her, even in a quiet and nonsubversive way.

Devon fingered the creased spines of a complete paperback collection of Stephen King. "I'd bet big money your mother comes here more than every six months, Jake. And she has incredibly broad tastes."

He answered with a grunt she interpreted as agreement, then thought the astonishment of learning something new and unexpected about his mother had knocked the wind out of him.

Good. Jake Tanner portrayed himself as a black-and-white kind of guy. She'd seen for herself that he drew lines and categorized people and situations even more than she did. Devon, at least, had learned from her sister and Darcy's loyal entourage of assorted nuts and crazies to be open-minded and not pin people with the most obvious label. She'd become a natural people watcher through her experiences with the wild world of rock and roll and her vocation as a writer. She figured that as a police officer, Jake practiced much the same technique. She wondered exactly how Jake had classified her when they'd first met and how he'd categorize her now.

That was easy, she realized. He saw her as an inexperienced lover, a popular writer who didn't have enough basic knowledge of attraction and seduction to contrive an erotic love story worthy of her name and talent. But he'd told her he'd instantly recognized an inherent sensuality about her, a feminine power she'd kept untapped.

Well, this afternoon she was going to not only prove him right, she was going to prove the student could also be the teacher.

"Why don't you keep opening windows and check out that old wall unit and see if it works?" she suggested, fanning herself. The cabin had to be at least ninety-five degrees with the windows open and the fan running, and while she had no objections to sweating with Jake, she certainly didn't want the cause to be poor circulation and a lack of Freon. "I'll look in the pantry. Maybe mix us up something cool to drink."

The cabin was well off the beaten path, in Homosassa Springs, and Devon hadn't noticed any neighbors as Jake had inched her SUV around the scrub pines, live oaks and palmettos nearly obscuring the dirt driveway. A little exploration revealed that the wood-and-tin structure had electricity, indoor plumbing and a freezer stocked with a couple of bags of ice and a relatively impressive supply of frozen sweets like bite-size chocolate-covered cheesecakes. She also found flour and pasta in tight-lidded glass jars in the refrigerator and a decent assortment of canned veggies and powdered drink mixes in the cupboard. After locating a pitcher in a cabinet and a couple of glasses, she mixed up a batch of lemonade and set it in the freezer to cool while she changed her clothes.

After airing out the cabin and establishing a comfortable temperature with the air conditioner, Jake had retrieved the packages from the car, including the paper bag Jillian had given him, and left them on the circa 1975 couch. Then he said he would check the condition of the canoe his father kept in the shed near the edge of the creek, fed, he said, by Homosassa Springs and connected to a smaller spring he'd forgotten the name of. He promised to return in a hurry, so Devon wasted no time in organizing her seduction.

She opened Jillian's gift first, marveling at the selection of shampoos, massage oils and lotions—all scented and flavored with lemons. A handwritten note explained that if not for the tart fruit, Jillian and Cade might never have met. Funny, but Jake hadn't mentioned anything about citrus in his version of their romance. Devon shrugged away her curiosity. Men never paid attention to details when it came to matters of the heart. Luckily, at the moment, the details didn't matter.

But Jillian's intentions meant the world to Devon. She instantly liked her, comparing her interference to something Sydney would do. Sly yet sexy, the gift basket could be a completely innocent addition to a guest bathroom...or it could be the impetus for one sensual afternoon.

Jillian Hennessy Lawrence might end up with a book dedicated to her if things worked out as Devon planned.

Choosing which undergarment to don wasn't hard, either, thanks to the lemon theme Devon seemed to be fortuitously building. When the saleswoman suggested the rather tame-looking nightie with impressionistic splotches of canary yellows and emerald greens, Devon had crinkled her nose. But when she'd learned about the tearaway bra cups, lace-up corset and crotchless panties hiding beneath the chiffon overlay, she'd changed her mind. She'd tossed it in the buy pile along with the faux leather T-back teddy, the sheer sapphire gown with the slit to the top of the thigh and a silky assortment of G-strings, bras and thongs that could be mixed and matched into over a dozen sexy ensembles.

But the color combination of the filmy short nightgown inspired her. Behind the paneled screen, she stripped out of her jeans and T-shirt, spritzed herself with a lemon-scented body splash from the gift basket, then quickly laced herself into the filmy chiffon.

Jake hadn't returned by the time she'd dressed, so she took the pitcher out of the freezer, added some ice, found glasses and a tray and set them on the ledge of the pass-through between the kitchen and the screened back porch. In a trunk she found a pine-green blanket, a little itchy from the wool blend but clean and soft and scented with cedar. Scooping up Jillian's basket with one hand and tucking the blanket under the other arm, she peered through the back door for a sign of Jake. She heard banging and bumping in the shed but couldn't see him or the structure through the trees. She did, however, spy a small but grassy clearing near the edge of the creek.

Perfect.

In less than five minutes, she had the scene set. Who said she didn't have the ability to construct an ideal setting for sex and seduction? She frowned, knowing the only person who'd made that claim had been her. Even Sydney had said Devon had it in her but was afraid to unleash her needs.

That may have been true two days ago, but it certainly no longer applied. She wanted Jake. And she intended to have him.

She retrieved the lemonade tray and was pouring when she heard Jake thrash toward the cabin on the other side of a thick hedge. She heard him call her name, softly at first and then with volume and force. With her back to the cabin, she sensed the moment he glanced out the window. She heard the squeak of the screen door as he stepped out of the house and padded toward her.

She didn't turn, but closed her eyes and enjoyed the

prickly reaction his proximity created on her skin. The strong scent of pine mingled with the lemons, creating a fresh, piquant perfume, intensified by the last few heated rays of the late-afternoon sun. The warmth burgeoned when Jake's boots broke a twig beneath the blanket.

"What's this?" he asked, his whisper stirring the tiny hairs across her neck. He tossed aside a towel he'd been using to wipe his hands and knelt beside her.

"A surprise." She lifted a glass of lemonade, sitting sideways as she turned to offer it to him. "You must be hot and thirsty after digging through that old shed."

He made no move to accept the drink, so she lifted the rim to his lips. Condensation made the glass slick and slippery. Desire nearly made her drop the tumbler.

He accepted her gesture and took a long swig, then swiped his tongue across his lips with a smooth smack.

"Hits the spot," he said, his gaze dropping slowly to the bare skin above her nearly nonexistent bodice. Twin triangles of sheer chiffon partially covered her breasts...and she knew that one quick tug could remove the material. But if she surrendered to the instinct to reveal the secret right away, she wouldn't accomplish her goal.

His pleasure first. At her hands.

She set the glass on the tray and pushed it to the

side, stretching on all fours like a lazy cat, well aware that the short nightie had fallen aside and that her barely covered backside undulated for his enjoyment.

She retrieved the lemon-flavored massage oil, twisted off the top and filled one palm with the slick lubricant. Turning, she rubbed her palms together. The oil, sitting in the sun, needed no warming. She just wanted him to know he would be first.

"I don't know about you, but my muscles weren't used to all that bouncing around," she said. "I could use a good massage."

He reached for the oil, but she blocked his path.

"Have you ever given a massage before?"

He shook his head. "It's not exactly brain surgery."

She chastised him with a pouty frown. "A whole bunch of massage therapists might be offended by that argument."

"Are *you* a certified massage therapist?" he asked, his tone skeptical despite his knowing expression.

With a grin, she rubbed the oil between her palms. "No, but I murdered one in my third book."

"And that makes you more experienced than me?"

She shrugged sweetly. "Maybe. Maybe not. I'm still the one with the oil all over my hands, and you're still the one who's overdressed."

He tore off his polo shirt quickly, and the sight of his bare chest glistening in the sunlight stole her breath. She'd seen him without a shirt before. She'd seen him fully nude. Maybe the newness hadn't yet

worn off. Maybe the magnificence of the man's phy-
sique would never fail to jump-start her heart.

"I thought I was supposed to be the one in charge."
His signature half smile caused an instant quickening
in her pulse.

"You can be," she admitted. "Soon enough. First,
lie down, get comfortable, and then you can do all the
instructing you want."

He did as she asked, but as he spread his body
across the blanket, she realized his jeans might get in
the way of her intentions.

"You need to loosen your pants."

"Loosen or remove?"

"You're the boss."

Jake chuckled, knowing he was no more the person
in charge of this scenario than she was an experienced
licensed masseuse. Still, he wasn't a man to argue
with a sexy woman in a wispy nightie, particularly
when she had slick, lemon-scented oil on her palms
and wicked intentions in her eyes.

The hedge his father had tried unsuccessfully to remove to clear the view to the water from the back
porch remained as thick and wild as ever. Jake stood
and removed his jeans and briefs, thankful that the
cabin, the clearing and this portion of the creek were
private and off the beaten path. He reclined facedown
on the blanket, shifting until the leaves and twigs underneath yielded a comfortable position. He wanted
to enjoy whatever Devon had in mind without distraction.

Boldly, she straddled his backside. For an instant, he thought he felt warm, moist flesh press into the curve of his spine, but he shook off the sensation the moment her hands made contact with his shoulders. She was, after all, wearing panties. He closed his eyes and conjured up a mental image of her lingerie. Bright colors. Lemon yellow and grass green. Thin straps curving over her shoulders. Triangles of sheer material barely covering her perfect breasts, the dark rose of her nipples obscured by swirls of color. But he'd seen the hard peaks and caught the fragrance of lemon dancing over her skin even before she poured the oil on her hands.

His mouth watered, reliving the sweet and tangy flavors of the lemonade. He wondered if she tasted the same way.

She pressed the oil, pungent, warm and slippery, into his flesh with surprisingly strong hands. She worked the muscles in his shoulders with short, rhythmic strokes, bearing down on him with her thumbs, soothing him with her palms. He shifted as an unfamiliar languor seeped into him. He couldn't resist emitting a satisfied moan.

"Not so bad for a rookie, am I?" she asked.

"You're a natural. I've said that all along."

Her hands left him, and without opening his eyes, he heard the squirt of oil, smelled the lemons, then relished the renewed pressure of her hands on his back. She traced his spine, inching backward and settling her weight on his thighs while she applied her silky magic.

Beneath her touch, he swelled with need. He shifted again, growing hard against the blanket. She was so close. He needed only to flip over to experience the euphoria of her slippery, skilled hands stroking him with the same loving attention she paid to every inch of his back.

She slipped down his body, sat on his knees and dipped her hands between his legs, then leaned forward and placed an open-mouthed kiss on the place where his spine met his hip bone.

"Devon," he said, her name a warning, but of what, he had no idea. Blood rushed through his body, dulling all his senses except the one that experienced the pleasure of her tongue swirling a tight circle on his skin.

"Yes, Jake?"

"Stop."

"Why? You're the one who packed Jillian's gift. Isn't this what you had in mind?"

She touched his thighs, then his hips.

Through a mottled haze of lust, he found the words. "Not exactly."

She stopped touching him, and he immediately cursed under his breath.

"Oh, that's right. You're the coach. You're supposed to be in charge. Well—" she moved off him "—those are the rules. It's too bad, though. I thought I'd add something new to our little game."

The minute he rolled onto his back and caught the mysterious, wanton glint in her eyes, he knew he'd be a fool to stop her. Somewhere in the back of his brain, somewhere beyond the pounding rush of need, he recalled he'd had some grand plan in orchestrating her education in the ways of eroticism. But who the hell was he kidding? Left to her own design, Devon had tipped the scales. She had something she intended to teach him about sensuality, and he couldn't wait to learn.

He hooked his hands behind his head and matched her grin.

"I'm *all* yours."

Her eyes flashed. "All?"

"I'm a man, Devon, not a monk. If you want to take over the game for an inning or two, I'm in no condition to argue."

She glanced down, exploring the full length of him with her eyes. "Maybe not, but you're in perfect condition for what I have planned, Jake." She swung her leg over him, flashing a glimpse of the open slit down the center of her panties. She settled her moist warmth on his belly, then replenished the oil on her hands. "So let's learn about sliding home."

11

Now she understood. The key to true eroticism was power. The power to entice. The power to deny. The power to withhold or award pleasure at any moment and for any reason. She never imagined she'd be the one wielding control. At least, not so soon...and not while with a potent man like Jake.

That was his gift to her, she realized, whether he knew it or not. If she could master a man like him, then she could control not only the fictional characters she wrote about but any lover she chose. She only had to accept what he offered—without reservations, fears or limits. She wanted him. All of him. And nothing was stopping her, nothing but a strong suspicion that once she'd learned him completely, once she'd pleasured him as completely as he'd satisfied her the night before, she'd never manage to walk away.

They'd only been together for two days, but still she cared about his future, ached for him when he told her tales of his childhood, surged with pride when he shared stories of tricky arrests and convictions. She couldn't help respecting a man who judged how he should treat her by his experiences with his sister—a woman he clearly adored—rather than comparing her to former lovers she'd yet to hear about and never cared to.

Her heart ached to let him in, to let the sparks of emotion flickering there burn into something stronger, but she had to resist. This affair was about sex, not love. Pouring oil on her hands, she forced herself not to think about anything more than here and now. If nothing else, she wanted to become the lover he judged all others by—his ideal.

With flattened palms, she drew a slick path to his waist, scooting onto his thighs so she had her balance when she slipped her hands around his sex.

"Oh, wow."

He was so thick, so hard. So deliciously male. So erotically strong. She stroked him slowly with a tight grip. She wanted to feel him inside her, stretching her, filling her. But waiting, giving him the delights he'd given her would make the joining more potent. It was this combination of anticipation and power, the elements of eroticism, Jake had forever branded into her, body and soul.

"See what you do to me?" he said, his voice raspy, deep.

"I intend to do much more."

She poured more oil, allowing a measure to dribble through her fingers onto him. "You know," she said, bending down, poising her mouth ever so close, "this is lemon-flavored oil, too." She licked, then moaned. "Oh, yeah. Tangy."

"Devon..."

Once she tasted him, he stopped talking. He groaned, he murmured, he tangled his hands into her hair, but said no words until he could take no more. Even after he tugged her free, she held him.

"Not so fast." She dug into Jillian's basket and retrieved the bright yellow square package she'd discovered under the straw cushioning. Her hands still slick with oil, she used her teeth to tear the condom packet open. The tiny circle glistened in the sunlight, sparkling with flecks of gold.

His eyebrows lifted high on his forehead.

"Let me guess," he ventured. "Lemon-flavored?"

She unrolled the latex over him with greased ease. "Made especially for use with the oil. According to the fine print, the little flecks of gold supposedly heighten a woman's pleasure." She added a layer of lubricant over the condom. "I'll let you know."

She snuggled down until the tip of his sex slipped between the parted fabric of her crotchless panties. The sensation jolted her, and she allowed a sweet sigh of pleasure to escape her lips.

His jaw slackened. "Your panties..."

"...have an opening just for you." She shifted to show him, and this time they moaned in unison. Hard to soft, she slid her moistened flesh against him, mimicking the movement of her oiled hands on his chest.

"You're driving me insane. You know that?"

She surged with the knowledge. "Want to see what else this fabulous nightie does?"

He didn't speak, and she witnessed the hesitation in

his eyes—a clear battle between desire and sanity. After wiping her oiled palms across his chest and shoulders, massaging as she spread the lubricant over his taut muscles and pounding heart, she reached up and unsnapped the triangles covering her breasts, tossing the bits of material aside. His eyes widened, then darkened to the most lustful shade of amber she'd ever seen.

With the material outlining her bare breasts and her nipples tight with need, Devon reached for the bottle of oil, then for Jake's hand. She poured a measure into his palm, then swirled the liquid with her finger before touching a thick droplet on each of her nipples.

"Now I taste like lemon, too."

He slapped his hands together, smearing the oil from one hand to the other. "Then I'll have to taste for myself."

The minute he pressed his hands against her breasts, Devon nearly jolted right out of her skin. Large and rough and warm, his palms and fingers wove an utterly awesome magic. He followed the triangular shape of the peekaboo bodice, coating her flesh with warmth and oil, gauging the weight of her and announcing his satisfaction with an appreciative groan. He paid particular attention to the darkening areolae, tracing and swirling the small, round shape. But he didn't touch her nipples except for a wayward scrape of a fingernail. She grew so tight, so hot with want, she arched her back in complete offering, pressing her mons into his sex, nearly climaxing, nearly losing herself in the burning combination of his body and hers.

Then he plucked her nipples, pinching her, squeezing her painfully hard and pleasuring her with sensations she'd never known. She must have cried out his name, because he answered with hers as he sat up and lifted her, soothing the aching flesh with his tongue.

Her eyes flashed open as she realized the fullness of her need for him, her need to experience every nuance of sexual exploration. His way. The electric rush of his play on her nipples pushed her into sensual overload. She wanted more.

"Again," she demanded.

His pupils dilated, and the blackness nearly swallowed her. She instantly recognized his chained desire, the carefully controlled hunger he could no longer check without paying a great price.

"No, that was too rough. I can't hurt you."

Her throat tightened. "Of course you can't hurt me, Jake. But what you just did felt amazing. Please, again."

He positioned his fingers on her nipples again, but with no pressure. "I won't hurt you," he repeated. His voice, rough with want, tinged with a quiver of uncertainty, tore at her heart.

She braced her hands on either side of his cheeks and forced his gaze into hers.

"I know."

With that, she folded her knees beneath her, combed her oil-slickened hands into his hair and waited. After a moment's hesitation, he squeezed again, flicking his tongue over her sensitive points, sending lightning bolts of unadulterated need to every part of her body. He braced one hand at the center of her back, holding her still while he used his mouth and teeth to repeat the commingled sensation of pain and sensual exhilaration until her entire body flamed.

Each time the pleasure jolted her, she cried out. He had to know, without question, that she wanted this torment. She needed to know the complete freedom of sexual release. She cupped her hands beneath her breasts and offered herself, pressing the flesh around her nipples tightly while he suckled her to near madness.

When the swirling cloud of lemon-lime chiffon got in his way, he tore it off. First the bodice, then the laces, until nothing remained but the panties, and those proved an inconsequential barrier to what they both wanted here and now. With one shift, he slid fully inside her. The condom's gold flecks prickled, stroking her like a thousand tiny fingertips. She barely had the clarity of mind to push him back, but she did until he stretched beneath her, his hands clutching her hips, his eyes hot.

She lifted slightly, then eased down, enthralled by the sensations. Instantly, the trees and sunlight started to spin. A wild rush of intoxication swept through her, ebbing momentarily so she could pull in a needed breath, then flowing like a torrential tidal wave the minute Jake added his hands to the mix, slipping his fingers between them. He touched and probed until she bucked and screamed his name, then he did the same with one long, deep thrust.

Suspended by the intensity, they remained locked together, panting, clutching, quivering. Devon had no idea how much time passed before Jake rolled them over on the blanket.

She fought to keep her eyes open while he turned her to the side and spooned his body to hers. She thrummed from head to toe, and though she'd just experienced the most intense orgasm of her life, she knew one touch would send her soaring again. She clenched her thighs, gasping when the throbbing renewed.

She tried to speak, but he urged her to remain quiet with a soft shushing sound.

"Ride the wave, Devon." He wrapped his arms around her. "There's no rush."

"I want you inside me again, Jake. God, I'm still on fire."

Hot tears burned her eyes the moment he reached between her thighs and slipped a finger inside her. She didn't want his hand. She wanted him. But he stole her ability to speak with his long, rhythmic strokes. All coherent thought fled her mind, replaced by the urgency of orgasm.

"I will be inside you again, Devon. Like this." He stretched her with a second finger, then a third. She nearly rolled onto her stomach, shamelessly allowing him full access. "You're so slick and hot. Let me slide you home one more time."

He found her clit and in moments he'd tipped her over the edge. She couldn't think. Could barely breathe. Even when he got off the blanket, covering her bare torso lovingly with his T-shirt, she couldn't find the words to ask him where he was going. Only one thought crossed her mind before she allowed the warmth of the evening, the sound of the creek and the contentment of complete sexual bliss to lure her to sleep.

When would he come back?

JAKE STRUGGLED into his jeans, leaving the zipper undone to avoid permanent damage. He couldn't believe what he'd done. He'd found a woman who was ready, willing and able to allow him complete, total and unhindered sexual release, and he was thinking about letting her walk away.

He knew she hadn't slept well last night, that she'd written like a madwoman this morning and that between shopping and traveling and off-roading, she had be exhausted. Still, she'd found the energy to construct a compelling and irresistible seduction. God, he wanted her. And not just sexually anymore, though his desire still pounded between his legs. When he'd probed her with his fingers, his cock had hardened to the consistency of a stone. He could have easily slipped inside her again and ridden the wave of pleasure with her. But he'd resisted, forcing her to orgasm alone.

Why?

He marched into the cabin, found the bottle of Southern Comfort he knew his mother hid in the top of the pantry behind the extra supply of candles and headed to the shed. Propping his butt on the side of an old iron drum, he unscrewed the cap and took a long swig. The alcohol, too sugary for his taste, nevertheless burned his throat and took some of the edge off his hard-on. He had to retain control of himself. If he'd followed his instincts and her entreaties, he would have made love to her that second time—and in the process would have lost more than he could give.

He wanted her so badly, with every fiber of what made him who he was, from his man-size pride right on down to that soft spot in his heart he thought no woman would ever touch.

But the minute she'd admitted she wanted her love-making wild, the moment she'd confessed that his roughness excited her, he realized he was in too deep.

She was all he wanted in a woman. All he'd ever wanted. How could he not want her? She was intelligent, strong, solid in her values and yet open to each and every experience he presented her with. She trusted him. She showed him that she knew with all her soul he'd never hurt her...and for the first time since he'd pounded that perp into a bloody pulp, he knew it, as well.

He'd feared he had a violent streak that was starting to finally reveal itself. He'd wondered if a lifetime of desperately trying to attain perfection, a childhood living under the roof of a man who demanded no less than spiritual supremacy despite his vicious fits of rage, had transformed him into an intolerable bully. He'd worried that his sexual fantasies about dominance and control were windows into a soul growing darker by the day. He'd agonized that all of the pent-up anger he'd harbored since childhood was finally rearing its ugly head.

But the dusky possibilities no longer seemed remotely probable. He had been able to control himself with Devon even after she'd encouraged him to unleash the restraints he'd built around his appetites. She'd forced him to face different aspects of his childhood, parts he'd forgotten after years of focusing only on his contentious relationship with his father. She reminded him of his love for his sister and his mother. She'd shown him that loving your family doesn't necessarily mean sacrificing yourself forever to their wants, needs or expectations.

She'd taught him when he was supposed to be teaching her. He only hoped the lessons he'd provided proved as valuable to her—valuable enough for her to abandon the one aspect of her plan he never expected to controvert.

She wanted their affair to be temporary. No strings. No falling in love allowed.

Well, he certainly was one for breaking the rules

lately, wasn't he? Because Jake Tanner most certainly did love Devon Michaels with every part of his soul.

Jake swore, polished off the rest of the Southern Comfort, accepting the liqueur wasn't going to dull his love for Devon any more than the dying sunlight would dim the intense Florida heat. He swatted a mosquito, realizing he shouldn't have left her in the clearing to be eaten alive by the bugs. He'd needed to get away and sort his thoughts, but the time for retreat was over.

And in typical Jake Tanner fashion, he had his concerns sorted, analyzed and concluded in record time. Thanks to Devon.

Trouble was, how did he tell her he was in love with her without scaring her away?

The basket from Jillian had obviously included several citronella candles, which Devon had lit sometime before or after she'd donned his T-shirt, then lain back to watch the play of sunset colors through the canopy of trees. He found her leaning on her elbows, a glass of lemonade in one hand, her hair swept up and secured with a strip of material salvaged from her nightie.

"Where'd you go?" she asked, scooting over so he had room to join her on the blanket.

"Had some thinking to do."

She acknowledged his answer with a murmur but didn't ask questions. He knew she was smart, but his estimation of her brilliance jumped. She apparently didn't want to push him about what he was thinking.

"What about you?" he asked. "What have you been up to since I've been gone?"

She lifted the lemonade and took a brief sip. "Well, I napped a bit." She stared at him in mock accusation. "Tried to recover some of my strength." Placing the glass beside the basket, she retrieved a pad of lemon-scented paper from Jillian's gift, along with a yellow pen topped with, of course, a lemon. "And I jotted down a few impressions of what just happened between us."

"Jillian included pen and paper?"

Devon grinned. "According to the Post-it note attached on the back, the suggested use was sexy love notes. I figured this was sort of the same thing. Do you want to hear what I wrote?"

Jake cleared his throat. "Actually, no."

"Really?"

He heard the offense and confusion in her voice, but what she'd scribbled on the paper probably had more to do with her fantasy life than with the situation they now faced.

"I don't want to read what you've written, Devon. Not yet. Maybe when the whole story is done, okay?"

She surveyed his expression through eyes as narrow as slits, but she shrugged and returned the paper to the basket. "So what now?"

"I love you."

She spun to face him, her mouth wide with surprise.

"Excuse me?"

Jake grumbled. Just like a woman to want to hear the confession twice.

"I said I love you, Devon."

She pressed her lips together tightly, then began collecting the remnants of her nightie and the half-empty bottle of massage oil. "Oh."

He watched her face in the dying light, but the shadows flickering from the candles made her guarded expression completely unreadable. Her silence did not convince him she didn't love him back— on the contrary. Jake knew Devon's capacity for love exceeded his. Maybe she'd fallen in love with him long before he had recognized the emotion in himself. She wouldn't want to accept her feelings for him or that her plan, her well-designed scheme for her independent future, would be blown away.

Or maybe she didn't love him at all. Maybe she had only seen him as a means to an end, a temporary lover who would instruct her in eroticism. But he didn't buy that scenario. He'd been a cop too long not to recognize true goodness, though that didn't mean she'd want to—or even should—put her needs on hold because he couldn't keep his emotions penned inside any longer.

"You don't have to say anything," he assured her, trying to snatch her hand but missing. "You don't even have to do anything. I just thought that since we've been honest with each other up to this point, I should tell you."

"Is that why you left? To decide whether or not to be honest?"

He shook his head. He'd been overwhelmed. And, frankly, scared. Of what she meant to him. Of how she might reject him once he told her the truth.

"I needed time to think."

"Maybe you needed time to think because you're not one hundred percent sure of your feelings, Jake." She crawled closer to him, her breath choppy, her eyes desperate. "We've only really known each other for a couple of days. We can't go making life-altering decisions simply because we have this awesome sexual chemistry."

Life-altering?

"How does admitting an honest feeling change your life?" Jake asked.

She didn't answer but continued cleaning up, clearing away evidence of their liaison, clues to what they'd just shared.

Damn. Jake grabbed her by the shoulders, stopped her rapid movements and explored the fear in her eyes. True and utter terror. He'd bet his bike that she loved him, but loving him didn't fit into her plan, did it? He hadn't considered, hadn't connected all the clues to realize what his admission could cost her.

Jake lightened the mood with a lopsided grin. "We do have great chemistry, don't we?"

She sighed with relief. "Yeah, we do. And we haven't even seen it all through." She slipped her hands over his shoulders and around his neck, snuggling close. "We've stolen home and we've slid home. Maybe there's a grand slam in our future? Our *near* future."

God, he wanted her. He was grateful he hadn't fastened his jeans. Jake's body surged with lust, particularly when she lowered her hand and stroked him. But it wasn't just lust anymore, was it? He wanted to join with her, connect with her...make *love* to her so deeply and thoroughly she'd forget everything else, all her goals, dreams, assumptions, in lieu of loving him.

But he knew she couldn't do that. No more than he could make love to her tonight. She'd lived her entire life with other people, taking care of other people. Until this weekend, she'd never had the chance to be on her own, and here he was laying his heart on the line and threatening what she perceived as her perfect future. He'd have to change her perception, but he couldn't do that overnight.

Using every ounce of his self-control, he eased her hand away. "No, Devon. No grand slams tonight."

She sat back on her feet with a huff, and although she opened her mouth to speak, she apparently changed her mind and pressed her lips together. Without another word, she finished packing up the basket, blew out the candles, dumped the glasses of lemonade into the bushes and disappeared into the cabin. He guessed she'd gone inside to change clothes and prepare for the ride home.

And not his home this time. Hers. He'd placed a

wedge between them, possibly ruined what could have been the best lovemaking he'd ever experienced, but he'd taken the chance he knew in his heart he needed to take.

He'd taken some time when he'd retreated to the shed, and Devon deserved the same space. Not too much space, he thought as he gathered the blanket and shook off the twigs and leaves. He'd already learned that she responded extremely well to anticipation and blossomed when she realized the potency of her power. He'd handed her the ultimate control over him—he'd handed her his heart. He only hoped that when he did slip back into her life, she would still want what he had to offer.

12

"YOU WHAT?"

Devon glanced over her shoulder, needing only one glimpse of Sydney's disapproving glare to send her scrambling under the laundry room sink, digging for the bucket she knew had to be there somewhere.

Unfortunately, she'd been friends with Sydney long enough to know that she could run but she couldn't hide. Not even under a sink. "I told him to go home, Sydney. Why is that so surprising to you? You're the one who told me I didn't have to fall in love with the man in order to have a hot affair with him."

Sydney slapped her hands on her black-spandex-encased thighs and let loose a string of four-letter words that would have made the local dockworkers proud. Devon shook her head. Cassie wasn't in the house anymore. The least she could do was allow Sydney full rein to vent her frustration—particularly since she'd hoped that washing her car would somehow provide a similar release for her.

The minute Sydney figured out that Devon was home, she'd jogged over and started pumping for information, peeking around corners and listening intently for any sign that sexy Jake Tanner was somewhere in the house. Devon finally admitted she'd sent him away the minute he'd brought her home, calling a taxi for him before she'd retreated to her office. She'd wanted to kiss him goodbye. She'd wanted to say something along the lines of, "See you tomorrow," or even, "Thanks for the memories." But the writer had no words, and the cop, apparently, had used up all of his in telling her he loved her, something she desperately hadn't wanted to hear.

Once he'd gone, she'd spent the entire night transcribing her handwritten notes and attempting, unsuccessfully, to reconstruct the ten pages she'd written on his laptop. The erotic words and sensual situations held little allure, however, without Jake close by to give them context. The characters from her new book refused to cooperate, walking through the scenes she'd constructed like cardboard cutouts with no life, no passion.

Devon had eventually gone to bed, not to sleep, but to toss and turn and wonder just how skillfully she'd been fooling herself over the past two days about the depth of her feelings for Jake.

Luckily, she had Sydney to answer her unspoken questions.

"Of course you don't *have* to love him but dammit, if you do, you're an idiot to let him walk away!"

"He didn't walk away," Devon reminded her, her voice breaking despite her effort to cover the sound. "I sent him away."

Sydney gestured, perhaps to berate her for quibbling about semantics, but no words came from her open mouth. Instead, she crossed her arms, took a deep breath and paused until she roped in her temper. "Devon, sweetie, what the hell are you thinking? You forget that I spoke with this man. He had the most charming way of telling me to mind my own business. A man with talent like that should *not* be dismissed."

Devon pulled the bucket out, slammed a handful of rags into it and tore open the storage cabinet to hunt for her favorite car deodorizer. The first order of business this morning had been to wash away all remnants of her trip into the wilderness with Jake. First the caked-on dirt and mud from the outside of the car, then the lingering musky scent of him from the inside. Then maybe, just maybe, she'd be able to cleanse her heart of all the hurt and regret.

"I have a lot of work to do today, Syd. I really don't feel like talking."

Talking and analyzing, even with her best friend, wouldn't change the one unalterable fact—she did love Jake. With all her heart. And that changed everything. Everything!

She pushed past Sydney into the kitchen, tugged on her worn Keds and grabbed the bucket, wincing when the heavy plastic slapped against her leg. She cursed, causing Sydney to wrench her by the arm to a violent halt.

"Why didn't you just tell him you love him?" Sydney asked. "You do, you know."

Devon rolled her eyes. "What difference would it make, Syd? I can't love him. I can't. Loving him means being with him, and being with him means never knowing what it feels like to be on my own." She surrendered to the overwhelming weakness assailing her limbs and leaned against the doorjamb. "He's so strong, so amazing. Intelligent. Witty. Full of secrets and mysteries I could spend a lifetime exploring. But I'm not eighteen. I know myself, and I wouldn't be able to resist putting his needs first even if he didn't ask me to. I'd spend all my time showing him, every minute of every day, that I cared for him more than anything in the world."

"Like you did for Cassie. Like you did for your mother. For everyone else in your life, including me."

Devon paused, then stalked out the side door and through the garage to the driveway that wound along the back, knowing Sydney would follow. "Precisely. It's my turn, Sydney. My turn to really be on my own."

Sydney flipped on the sunglasses she'd hooked at her neckline. "The downside is that being on your own, to you, also means being alone. What if you don't like that feeling? You've never really experienced it. I, on the other hand, am once again the expert. And believe me, darlin', loneliness, unlike great sex, is not something I recommend to the people I love."

Devon unwound the hose, filled the bucket with soap, then attached the sprayer and began zapping the encrusted mud and dirt off her truck. She wished the whooshing sound of the water had drowned out Sydney's confession, but she'd heard every word and taken each to heart. Once again, her friend was right. Devon didn't know what it felt like to be completely alone. But, dammit, horrible or not, she wanted a chance to find out if she could handle life on her own with only her paycheck to support her, her wit and intelligence to make the right choices for *her*.

She'd have no one's welfare to consider except hers. For so long, she'd coveted such selfishness, her desire spurring her to work harder, write faster. If not for her single-minded focus, she might never have pursued Jake in the first place, no matter how much he made her heart flutter or piqued her sexual curiosity. How could she throw it all away without at least giving independence a try?

"I can't always take your recommendations, Sydney. The time has come for me to start making decisions on my own, based on my own knowledge. Right or wrong, I have to see this through."

Sydney twisted her mouth into a doubtful frown, then cautiously padded over and pulled Devon into a quick and efficient hug. Anything more and they'd both start bawling, and they knew each other well enough to avoid moments like that at all costs. "Well, I hope you know what you're doing."

"Yeah, me, too."

Devon turned to her task, focusing on the immediate goal—a good washing of her beloved vehicle.

When she'd requested a place to wash her car, she should have guessed Darcy would have her contractor build a fully automatic station, with two brick walls on either side, a tiled roof to match the house and attractive roll-down doors to protect the equipment when not in use. All Devon really needed was a bucket, some soft clean rags, gentle dish soap and a hose. Still, she liked the shade the station provided, and the privacy. With a good quarter acre between the car wash and the tall fence that surrounded their property, she was completely isolated from the world.

Once she passed through the tall iron gates emblazoned with two huge Ds—one for Devon and one for Darcy—she entered a private, separate world. The house and the grounds had, at first, been her sanctuary from the prying eyes of the media and celebrity hunters looking to exploit her niece or her sister. But Devon had made the place a home, a vast expanse of safe space for Cassie to grow and for her to hone her skills as a writer. Just two days ago, she'd intended to use the advance money from her new erotic novel to buy the house and transform it, even if only in her own mind, into a symbol of her independence.

Yet since watching Jake the night before from her upstairs window as he waited for the taxi, she wondered if the house was a self-imposed prison, meant to protect her from risking her heart. Her mother, her sister, Cassie and even Sydney—Devon could love them all freely, confident that they'd return the sentiment no matter what. But what about Jake—or any man, for that matter? He might love her now, but what about tomorrow? How would he feel about her when the passion wasn't so absolutely perfect? When he knew every nuance of what pleasured her? When no discoveries remained?

Then she realized she needed to answer a more vital question. Was she grappling with a quest for independence, locking herself away from love? Walking away before any man had the chance to abandon her first?

She sighed, aware that Sydney must have returned to the house. Devon focused on her task, never expecting Sydney to help. She'd probably gone to the house to pop open a diet soda and catch up on her reading until Devon returned.

As she glanced toward the house, Devon spied a shadow on the other side of the sport utility vehicle. Leaning on a brick wall near the spigot, dressed in worn jeans and a navy-blue T-shirt, Jake watched her with the most serious expression she'd ever seen on his face.

She released the sprayer handle, cutting off the water and filling the covered area with nothing but the sound of dripping, draining water, keeping time with the pounding of her heart.

"How'd you get in?" she asked.

She did, after all, live in a secure gated community.

"Showed the guard my badge."

"I thought you were on suspension."

His smile lacked any real humor. More for show

than substance, she figured. "Was. Till this morning. My lieutenant called. I received a reprimand, was ordered to attend an anger management course. But I'm back on duty, if I want."

"If you want?"

This wasn't the first time she'd heard Jake refer with uncertainty to his job, but now that he'd been reinstated to active duty with nothing more than a slap on the wrist, she couldn't help wonder about his reluctance. Then there was the question of why he'd returned to her house.

Devon didn't deny that she'd pulled a major retreat the day before. She'd experienced what amounted to emotional overload, spawned by a huge dose of fear. Jake had proclaimed his love for her, and whether or not they'd been involved for two years or two days, she knew the significance of his words. He wasn't a man to share his emotions without great thought and strong conviction. He loved her. She believed him. But the truth remained—she couldn't let his emotions dictate the direction of her life.

Devon slipped the sprayer onto a hook on the wall, grabbed a rag from the bucket and wrung it from sopping to damp. She'd added too much soap to the mix, making the water slick, reminding her of the massage oil they'd spread all over each other just the day before. She shook her head. She couldn't afford to let her mind wander in that direction. She couldn't afford to have him here, period. Not if she intended to remain true to her plan—to experience true independence for the first time in her life. Not if she had any hope of escaping the trap her love for him lured her toward, like fresh meat in a steel snare to an animal starving for food.

"I guess both of us still have some serious thinking to do," he answered.

She bit her bottom lip, trying to keep from revealing how seriously she'd been thinking about him since the moment he left. She'd concluded that she loved him, that she wanted to spend the rest of her life with him. That she'd gladly give up her dream of independence and her lessons in self-reliance to spend more time in his arms.

But she refrained from telling him, well aware of how ridiculous her declaration would sound, how it contradicted everything she wanted for herself and her future. She'd only known him, *really* known him, for two days. Wasn't it more likely she was latching on to him as a means to keep from being lonely? Allowing her overloaded libido to dictate the direction of her life?

Sydney had been right—Devon had never experienced living on her own, being by herself in the big house and taking care of her needs first and foremost. Still, loneliness wasn't so foreign to her. What about the countless times she'd been surrounded by a crowd of people, interacting with them and honestly enjoying herself but still feeling as if no one existed who truly understood the way her mind worked or how deeply in her heart she harbored her hopes and dreams?

But Jake understood. At least, he tried to. He'd brought her the laptop and left her alone for an entire morning, somehow knowing that she needed to work. He'd taken her shopping, practically ordering her to purchase the sexy, feminine underthings she'd always admired but never had the guts to buy. And in an open, breathtaking clearing on the edge of the Florida wilderness, he'd transferred the ownership of her seduction from him to her, giving her the reins yet still making sure she experienced complete pleasure.

And, most of all, he'd told her he loved her, knowing his admission would likely send her running until she could sort through her conflicting feelings.

Which, unfortunately, she hadn't yet done. She couldn't separate what was real from the possible romantic musings of a woman who made her name and reputation with her imagination.

"I do still have a lot of serious thinking to do, Jake. I just want to know, what you said, what you admitted…"

"That I'm in love with you?"

Even casually spoken, the words spawned a shivery tingle up her spine and cracked another bit of the casing she'd built around her heart. "Yes, that. I'm…honored. That you could feel that way about me after so short a time…"

He stepped toward her, and Devon used all her physical strength to keep herself rooted to the spot.

She wouldn't run from him, or to him. No matter how tall or large or handsome or amazing he was. No matter how enticing the prospect of falling into his embrace would be.

No matter how much she loved him.

"You think I've fallen in love too fast?" Jake asked.

"No! Yes. I don't know. I've never been in love before, Jake. I really don't know what it is...what it means. I'm trying to be honest with you, with myself." She slammed the rag into the bucket, sending a geyser of soap bubbles and water into the air, splashing her legs. She swore under her breath and swiped away a trail of foam. "Let's just chalk it up as one more thing Devon Michaels doesn't know a damned thing about."

Jake retrieved the rag from the bucket, wrung it, then knelt beside her. He smoothed the damp terry cloth, soft from the fresh, soapy water, down her leg. "I never signed on to teach you about love, Devon. In the love department, I'm a total rookie."

She chewed her lip as his ministrations sent shock waves of wet desire all over her body. "You're quite the expert in the *making* love department."

He rewarded her compliment with one of his disarming half grins. "Maybe. Maybe not. But I was thinking this morning that I do still owe you one more lesson. All I need is for you to pretend you love me back."

Devon swore, the harshness of the words mangled

by the quiver in her voice, a subtle shaking spawned by the feel of the towel on her skin.

He glanced at her, his determination in the line of his jaw, in the intensity of his amber gaze. "Come on, Devon. Use that imagination of yours."

When he reached her ankle, he reversed direction and wiped upward, curling the towel around the back of her leg so the sensations of wet, soapy warmth aroused the soft inside of her knee, the sensitive flesh of her thigh.

"We talked about a grand slam yesterday," he continued, tickling, teasing her skin with the towel. "What could give a bigger payoff than sex between two people who are in love?"

"Jake...this...isn't a good idea."

"Why? Because it feels so good? So right?" He leaned forward and kissed her below the hem of her shorts, then reached across to dampen the towel again. This time, he didn't wring it dry, but instead sloshed slick suds all over her skin.

"Yes...no."

She had to brace her hands on his powerful shoulders to keep from losing her balance. God, she wanted him. Just as he described. Love out in the open. Nothing to hide. Since the first moment she'd seen him, long before her book deal had come into play, long before they'd made the stupid, selfish deal to engage in an exclusively sexual relationship, she'd known he'd been the type of man she could give her heart to. A man who wouldn't throw such a precious gift away.

"Decide, Devon." He shifted, balancing on both knees as he targeted a hot kiss on her belly through the flimsy fabric of her nylon shorts. "Even if you walk away from what we've started, do you really want to do that before you've had it all? I don't. I love you. Let me show you. All of you."

She couldn't protest when he lowered her shorts and panties in one quick swipe. She couldn't run when he leaned back long enough to take off his shirt and fling it beside a puddle. A quick glance toward the house revealed that even if Sydney had decided to stick around until after Jake left, which Devon doubted, she wouldn't be able to see anything unless she came looking—and Sydney undoubtedly knew they needed privacy.

They were alone. Devon. Jake. Their desire. Their love. Even if she couldn't acknowledge the emotion out loud, she could show him. She could allow herself to be shown.

"I want you, Jake. I won't deny that. Ever."

She tore her T-shirt over her head and unclipped her bra while she kicked off her Keds. His jeans and sneakers disappeared just as quickly, leaving them both exposed to the shaded sunlight, to each other.

The air seemed to bend under the weight of the atmosphere. Trapped heat. Steaming water. Then Jake's whiskey-colored eyes lightened with mischief, alleviating the oppressiveness.

"We could both be arrested for indecent exposure."

Instantly, she remembered his classroom fantasy.

She'd wanted to make that scenario come true for him but hadn't had the opportunity. Until now.

She turned and placed her hands on the brick wall, leaning forward and spreading her legs as a criminal would before a body search. "Time for my pat down?"

Jake groaned but complied. He slid behind her, his erection taut, his body dry and hot against her wet warmth.

"We should have a soft bed, satin sheets," he protested. "A condom."

"There's a condom in your wallet," she replied, having spied the foil packets when he'd taken his credit card out at Frederick's of Hollywood the day before.

"If we're pretending we're in love, we should take this inside. Make it special, intimate. We've had wild sex. Now we should do it right."

Devon turned, leaning her backside on her hands, drawing up one knee and placing her bare foot against the hard, hot brick. "Jake, you don't have to be valiant with me. You can check your chivalry and impossible perfection at the door. It's just us. A chance to make real the fantasy you've shared only with me. I want to make it come true for you. Beds and satin sheets are wonderful, but that's not really us, is it? We're about what's raw, what's basic." She kicked off the wall, snagged the bucket, then plopped it down at his feet. If the man got any more gallant, any more noble in her eyes, she'd never, ever be able to let him go.

She dipped down and pulled the clean washcloth out of the cool, soapy water, allowing a long stream to drip down, sloshing them both with water and suds. "I used to think satin sheets and rose petals were key ingredients to what was erotic, and maybe they are...sometimes. But we've made some fine memories with blindfolds, wool blankets and lemon massage oil. Now we've got a brick wall, a water hose, some very slick soap. This is about a grand slam, remember?"

She pressed the sopping rag to his chest, wincing with him when the cold sensation met with his hot flesh. He closed his eyes and took a deep breath, which she interpreted as her invitation to finish what she'd started. He'd awarded her the power yet again, and the burst of self-confidence proved no less intoxicating now than it had the day before.

She washed him slowly, her mouth drying as the water and soap glided over his skin. In the daylight, she watched, fascinated, as his muscles bunched and coiled in response to her touch, as his skin prickled and warmed. She followed the trail of the cloth with her hands, touching every sinew of his chest, every curvature of his arms and abs.

Before she washed him completely, she replenished the water and soap on the rag.

She started with his thighs, then worked her way up, cupping his soft sacs with the cloth, then sliding the moisture over his long, hard length. He blew out a breath, then quickly inhaled, bringing her attention to his face. His expression was guarded, tight.

She dropped the rag in the bucket and took him in her palm, drawing as close to him as she could while she stroked him, transferring a layer of soap and water onto her skin, moistening the tips of her nipples. "You are so hard. I can't wait to feel you inside me."

"Devon..."

"Shh."

She slipped around him without letting go, retrieved the rag and doused his back, never once slowing her rhythmic massage. He grew even longer, even harder, spawning a potent thrill throughout her body. She pressed her breasts to his back and snuggled close.

His surrender ended with a quick turn, and in an instant the wet rag was in his possession, her back flattened against the cool steel of her car door, her body raging with wild need.

"You're not playing with water and soap, Devon. You're playing with fire."

Jake hadn't come to Devon's house to seduce her. He hadn't misused his badge to gain entrance to her gated community in hopes of being seduced. He'd returned this morning only to give her the diskette she'd left in his laptop, the same one crammed into the back pocket of his discarded jeans. At least, that was what he'd told himself.

But the truth was, he was a man who finished what he started. No matter how much he wanted Devon in his life for the long haul, her goals, her independence were important to her. So they were important to him. If she insisted on walking away, she needed to have full and complete knowledge of what she'd be missing.

He dipped the rag in the water and proceeded to wash her, starting with her breasts.

"Mmm...I'll have to play with fire more often," she cooed, her eyes heavy-lidded, her lips pouty and moist.

"Only with me, Devon," he vowed, then placed a long, luxurious kiss on her mouth. He knew such a statement might send her running, but he didn't care. Honesty had been important between them from the start. He wouldn't change that.

He lowered his kisses to her neck as he lowered the saturated towel down her belly.

"I can't promise, Jake."

He didn't stop washing her, kissing her, touching her. "Yes, you can. Because after you feel me inside you this one last time, knowing how much I love you, you won't ever want another man."

"You're some kind of arrogant, you know that?" she asked, her sapphire eyes blazing.

He chuckled, then slipped the towel between her legs. Her breath caught, then she panted harder, heavier, as if the air couldn't fully enter her lungs so long as he touched her so intimately.

"I have every reason to be. I love you."

Until Devon, Jake hadn't thought of himself as a

great lover. He was a guy, and he'd made some women come. Big deal. But with Devon, his seduction took on a higher significance. Not because of her book deal or the knowledge she'd asked him to give her, but because he wanted to pleasure her more than anything else in the world. His needs easily took a back seat, and yet she found a way to cater to him at the same time. Like here, against the car. Standing up. Hot and ready.

He kissed her long and hard, stopping only when she was nearly breathless to retrieve the condom and put it on. Slick hands made the task difficult, but Jake triumphed, returning to her before the bubbles coating her skin had dispersed.

Guiding one of her legs onto the step-up bar, Jake pressed into her soft folds. Their bodies, slick from the soap, slid together from head to toe. He locked his hands with hers to keep her from slipping away. Her tightness slowed him down, but when she wrapped her leg around his waist and practically climbed onto him, he knew his ability to control their lovemaking had sloshed away with the soap and water.

She wanted him. He wanted her. He loved her. She loved him, he felt certain. That knowledge blasted everything else away. Each cry from her lips urged him deeper. Each moan from his throat made her hold on tighter.

Climax came fast and loud and furious. Together, in sync, like they had been since that first kiss in the stairwell. She wrapped her arms around his neck, locked both legs around his middle, her mouth glued to his with desperate need. He turned them, using his back against the car to anchor their passion until the sensations subsided, until his erection went lax and her muscles unclenched. Gently, softly, like an errant stream of foam, she slipped away.

Silently, she unhooked the hose, adjusted the spray nozzle and washed herself clean of dirt from the car and foam from the rag. She handed him the hose, barely looking him in the eye. He washed away the soap, then, determined to undo an uncomfortable moment, turned the stream on the car.

He had the entire sport utility vehicle cleared of mud and ready for washing before she joined him, dressed in her wet T-shirt and shorts. Poised in her hand was the rag he'd just used to wash away her reluctance to love him. He dressed, grabbed a second towel and replenished the soap and water in the bucket. By the time the Escalade was shiny and dry, they still hadn't spoken a word.

He helped her gather her things, tossing the rags into the blue plastic pail. She knelt beside it. He joined her.

She bit her bottom lip. "You know I do love you, Jake. I just wish I knew what that meant. Because until I do, I can't make any promises."

"That's where you're wrong, sweetheart. You just made a promise to me. Right there, in my arms, up against your car."

She groaned, more from frustration than any sense

of humor, he realized. "That may be, but I have no idea what I promised you."

He reached across and stroked her cheek, still damp, still flushed from his touch. "That's okay. Remember what I said about the power of anticipation? I've learned to be a patient man. I'll wait while you figure it out."

____Epilogue____

IN WHAT amounted to a cherished ritual, Devon placed both her hands palms down on the box in front of her, ignoring the sounds of the lunch crowd at the tables around her. She didn't have to say a prayer this time—the book had long ago been accepted, the large advance check earning interest in her checking account. But after six months of writing and one set of minor, plot-focused revisions, her first hardcover erotic novel—aimed at making Devon Michaels a household name—would soon start its journey to New York.

It was all thanks to a rogue cop named Rolf Anderson, who'd injected her lead character, private investigator Leah Lucas, with just enough erotic power and anticipation to make their interactions unbelievably incendiary.

Of course, after six months with Jake, Devon not only believed in incendiary, she figured they'd made great strides toward reinventing the word.

After huffing out a breath of relief, Devon stuffed the manuscript into her tote bag, then signaled the waiter to her tall round table in the back of the Tex-Mex restaurant's bar. She checked her watch, noting she had only about thirty minutes before the first session of her new fiction writing class at the University of South Florida. Just enough for her to complete the ceremony she and Sydney had inadvertently invented years ago when they were unpublished writers struggling toward that first big sale.

She snuggled into her sweater, knowing she should order something hot rather than the required frozen margarita. But she didn't mess with superstitions. One toast to the person who most influenced the book, then she'd drop the manuscript off at the nearest post office, hope for the best and warm up later.

She checked her watch again. Where was Jake?

"So, what's your pleasure?"

Devon grinned, turning slowly toward the voice she knew belonged to Jake.

"Margarita, frozen."

"Strawberry?"

"Classic."

Jake barked the order to the bartender, who immediately complied. Man, oh man, this guy could run the world if he set his mind to it.

He slid onto the tall bar stool with ease, looking particularly dashing in the leather bomber jacket she'd bought him for Christmas.

"Don't you have a class to teach in a half hour?" Jake asked.

Devon fingered the soft leather, impressed. She knew she'd discussed her schedule with him but hadn't expected him to remember details, not with all the turmoil raging through his life. While Jake and she had spent the past six months together—dating like a normal couple, then making love like the last two adults in existence on earth—he'd been struggling with his job. He'd changed departments twice, even taking on the role of resource officer at a troubled local high school in hopes of rediscovering his inherent love for police work.

Devon had been so wrapped up in her writing, she didn't know what he'd decided to do—which had been fine with him. Just like she'd had to learn about living on her own, Jake insisted he had to make up his mind about his career on his own. When she'd called him a few days ago to announce she'd finally finished her revisions and had typed "The End," he'd hinted he had finally decided on another change, one he intended to make permanent.

"First day of class." She patted her stomach, which did a little apprehensive flip. "I always get a little nervous. The margarita will be doing double duty. Calming me down and celebrating this book."

As if on cue, the waiter delivered the drinks, served in frosty mugs and garnished with salt and a wedge of lime. Devon plucked out the straw and lifted her mug. Jake did the same.

"To you, Jake Tanner. My inspiration. My teacher. And the best lover a woman could ever have."

Jake's half grin, coupled with a slight blush, stole her breath. He lifted his drink to her.

"To you, Devon Michaels. The most amazing

woman I've ever met. My inspiration, my teacher—"
he cleared his throat "—and definitely the most adventurous, giving lover a man could ever dream of."

They clinked glasses, and the sound signified so
much to Devon, she could barely steady her hand to
raise the drink to her lips. She'd accomplished all
she'd set out to do—and Jake had given her the time
and space to work things out on her own. She didn't
figure six months was the most significant amount of
time a woman with her history could spend relying
on herself and living a relatively self-centered, independent life, but six months would have to do. She
wasn't getting any younger. Jake hadn't made any
move to change their arrangement, but she knew in
her heart the time had come.

She took a big, cold swallow of the tangy drink,
smacked a layer of salt off her lips with her tongue
and then reached into her purse. She took out a small
jeweler's box and placed it in front of him.

He eyed her skeptically. "What's this?"

"Open it."

He palmed the box, and Devon nearly choked on an
invisible lump in her throat. Never, not since the book
she'd given Jake a half year ago, had she taken such a
risk. But that's what strong, independent women did,
didn't they? Took life and love into their own hands?

Jake popped back the top, his expression bewil-
dered. He met her expectant stare with an unreadable
look.

"Read the note," she said. "I seem to do much better with the written word."

He flicked a small square of paper out of the top. She closed her eyes, having memorized the message she'd finally settled on after nearly fifty unsuccessful drafts.

He'd once told her he'd applied the Keep It Simple, Stupid principle when charting her education in the erotic. She'd borrowed his mind-set and had written only two words.

"Marry me."

He spoke the words, then paused until she opened her eyes.

"Is that a question, or are you just reading out loud?" she asked.

He pulled out the matching set of sapphire-studded bands. "I always thought I'd be the one doing the asking. You've muddied the waters."

She leaned forward, longing for another shot of frozen tequila but wanting to feel his hands in hers even more. "Does it matter who asks whom? I want to spend my life with you, Jake. All of it. Every minute."

The rapid pounding of her heart caused her hands to shake. He flipped his fingers around hers and held her steady. "Every minute? You might not get much work done."

She sighed. "You know what I mean. Marry me, Jake."

He pulled her forward and kissed her, long and hard, nearly knocking over her drink, his drink, the rings and the table. When they broke, everyone in the crowded bar applauded. Perhaps she'd spoken a little louder than she'd intended.

They laughed, waved, then retreated into a silent, private world, despite the cheers and the bartender's announcement that their drinks were on the house. Jake took out a generous tip, downed half his drink in one gulp, then snagged the rings and knelt at her feet.

"My turn."

He slid the smaller band onto her finger, then gave her the other to put on his. He stood, kissed her again, inspiring another round of rowdy congratulatory wishes.

"Devon, I want you to be my wife. But—" he held up his hand before she could agree "—you need to know something first. I'm quitting the force."

She grinned, having long suspected he'd come to this conclusion. He was an exceptional cop, a devoted public servant. But the realities of justice, the fact that the bad guys sometimes got away or that they forced such horrific damage on the innocent before he could stop them had been chipping away at his devotion to law enforcement. He'd used these last six months to search his soul for a solution, and apparently, judging by the twinkle in his whiskey irises, he'd found one.

"I suspect, from that look in your eye," she concluded, "that you aren't planning on letting me bring home the bacon."

He rolled his shoulders in an adorable shrug. "You've taken care of enough people in your lifetime.

It seems my sister, Kat, has found yet another new profession in Los Angeles, one she's not only good at, but one I think she'll stick with. She's an assistant producer for a new television series that will be filming here in Tampa. An undercover cop series. They need a consultant and will be paying big bucks. I also have my eye on another profession, but it can be very fickle. Could be years before I make one dime."

Devon chuckled. "Sounds like writing."

He matched her laugh with a devastating grin. "That's because it is."

"What?"

He dipped his hand into her tote bag, where her class roster had been peeking out of a slick green folder. "You haven't even looked this over, have you?"

She took the computer-generated listing from him. No, she hadn't read it. She'd been too wrapped up in finishing her book to look at a list of names that wouldn't mean anything to her until she had faces to match them with.

There, third to the last. *Tanner, Jake.*

"You're taking my writing class?"

He folded his arms across his chest. "Fair is fair. I taught you. Now you can teach me. You see—" he lifted her tote bag and helped her collect her things "—I heard there was going to be an opening in the mystery genre, what with you shifting over to the best-seller category."

He led her toward the door, completely ignoring

the shock and expectant surprise that kept her from saying one word. She suspected he was kidding, but she certainly didn't care. He helped her into her jacket, the black leather one he'd bought her for Christmas—yet again proving that the two of them usually thought along the same lines.

"Actually, Kat suggested she and I work on some novelizations for the series, but I can't rely on my sister to do all the writing. And though I have loads of police knowledge, I have no idea how to put a novel together. So I signed up for your class. Might as well learn from the best."

After they walked into the crisp sunlight of a typical Florida winter day, Devon jerked him to a stop. A chilled breeze nipped at her skin but did nothing to halt the increasing warmth in her belly.

"Do you really want to write, or are you just making an excuse for us to spend more time together?"

She was happy either way, but the leap from cop to writer seemed so huge, she wanted to understand the path of his logic. Some things never changed.

"I've been toying with the idea for a while. I used to write stories as a kid, just like you. So when you mentioned in *my* class that cops and writers think alike, and that my cold cases could spark some interesting ideas, writing seemed like a new challenge. You don't mind, do you? Me stepping into your domain?"

She flung her arms around his neck and pulled herself up to give him a big smack of a kiss on the mouth. "Personally, I like it when you step into my domain."

She winked, knowing Jake would read the naughtiness in her tone. "I can think of all sorts of interesting ways to motivate your writing. But you should be forewarned. I'm a tough teacher."

Jake pulled her into an embrace, curling his massive body around her and cocooning her with a heat she suspected could easily last a lifetime. "I've heard. I did tell you that I wanted my first mystery to have some great sex in it, right? The homework alone just might kill me."

Right before he kissed her again, this time with that painful, drawn-out laziness that had been her first lesson in the power of anticipation, Devon murmured, "Yeah, but what a way to go."

* * * * *

Wait! The fun's not over yet.
Watch out for Sydney's story,
coming in early 2003
from Temptation.

magazine

♥───────────────────── **quizzes**

Is he the one? What kind of lover are you? Visit the **Quizzes** area to find out!

♥───────────────── **recipes for romance**

Get scrumptious meal ideas with our **Recipes for Romance**.

♥───────────────── **romantic movies**

Peek at the **Romantic Movies** area to find Top 10 Flicks about First Love, ten Supersexy Movies, and more.

♥───────────────────── **royal romance**

Get the latest scoop on your favorite royals in **Royal Romance**.

♥───────────────────────── **games**

Check out the **Games** pages to find a ton of interactive romantic fun!

♥───────────────── **romantic travel**

In need of a romantic rendezvous? Visit the **Romantic Travel** section for articles and guides.

♥───────────────────── **lovescopes**

Are you two compatible? Click your way to the **Lovescopes** area to find out now!

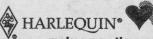

HARLEQUIN®

makes any time special—online...

HINTMAG

Blaze

The Trueblood, Texas
tradition continues in...

HARLEQUIN® *Blaze*™

TRULY, MADLY, DEEPLY
by Vicki Lewis Thompson
August 2002

Ten years ago Dustin Ramsey and Erica Mann shared their first
sexual experience. It was a disaster. Now Dustin's determined
to find—and seduce—Erica again, determined to prove to
her, and himself, that he can do better. Much, *much* better.
Only, little does he guess that Erica's got the same agenda....

Don't miss Blaze's next two sizzling Trueblood tales,
written by fan favorites Tori Carrington and Debbi Rawlins.
Available at your nearest bookstore
in September and October 2002.

TRUEBLOOD, TEXAS

HARLEQUIN®
Makes any time special ®